REALLY-TRULY Stories

Book 6

By Gwendolen Lampshire Hayden

Illustrated by Vernon Nye

TEACH Services, Inc.
PUBLISHING
www.TEACHServices.com • (800) 367-1844

Copyright © 2013 TEACH Services, Inc.
ISBN-13: 978-1-4796-0114-1 (Paperback)
ISBN-13: 978-1-4796-0115-8 (ePub)
ISBN-13: 978-1-4796-0116-5 (Kindle/Mobi)

Library of Congress Control Number: 2012955985

Published by

TEACH Services, Inc.
P U B L I S H I N G
www.TEACHServices.com • (800) 367-1844

Table of Contents

Dedication

This book is lovingly dedicated to my sister Stephanie Lampshire Thompson, and to Mrs. Bessie B. White, whose many kindnesses to our family have been much appreciated throughout the years.

Walter Carefully Tiptoed Down the Narrow Back Stairs
That Led to the Big Clock in the Main Hallway

Chapter 1
A Canadian Christmas

CAN you see what mamma's doing now? Oh, I can hardly wait to find out what we're going to get for Christmas!" As John's breath swirled frostily upward in the bedroom's icy air he clenched his teeth to keep them from chattering.

"Do you s'pose we'll really get our wind-up trains this year, Walter?"

"S-sh! I've told you a hundred times I don't know any more about it than you do. But you'd better be quiet or mamma and papa'll hear us."

The two boys silently pushed themselves away from the small stovepipe floor opening in the corner of their bedroom and crept stealthily across the bare floor toward their bed.

"Just listen to Dave and Wilfred snore!" Walter exclaimed. "You'd think they'd stay awake too and try to find out what they're going to get for Christmas. But maybe they aren't so anxious as we are. Dave's already got his wind-up train, and Wilfred's too little for one yet."

"I thought sure I'd get a peek at some of the presents mamma was setting on the table," John mourned. "I wanted to see what she was going to put by my plate. I can hardly wait till morning to find out.

"Br-r-r!" shuddered John when Walter slipped in beside him, pushing him into the icy wastes at the back of the bed. "Why can't you sleep next to the wall for just once?"

"Because I'm two years older than you, even if I'm not any bigger," Walter retorted, "and I want this place. But don't talk now. The folks are right by the stove, and they'll be sure to know we're awake. Papa looked up at the ceiling once or twice while I was watching, but he didn't see us. You know they always want our presents to be a surprise."

As the boys curled under their warm quilts they watched the faint reflection of the kitchen light shining through the little floor opening in the corner of their bedroom. Usually the kitchen was dark and deserted at this hour of the night, for their Canadian winter bedtime came early, and was welcomed gratefully by the hard-working Neufeld family. However, the boys knew that on Christmas Eve there was sure to be yellow lamplight blooming on the long table, while reddened flickering gleams from the eyelets of the huge black kitchen stove slanted out into the room's dark corners.

John felt his tense muscles gradually relax as their chilled bedding gradually became warm and cozy. Pleasant little prickles ran up and down his spine while he lay wide-eyed in the December blackness and thought eagerly of Christmas morning, so near and yet so far away. He thought also of Christmases past when he and Walter, Dave and Wilfred, had lain flat on their lean stomachs and had taken turns peering eagerly down onto the long oilcloth-covered kitchen table. He remembered that sometimes they had gotten exciting glimpses of gifts, but sometimes they had been able to see nothing at all of the many good things to be revealed at breakfast time.

In the wintry stillness John thought of their large family and of all the presents that mamma and papa had to get ready every Christmas for each member of the happy three-in-one Neufeld family. First of all came papa's list. Mentally he named each one, beginning far back with the six children born to papa and to papa's first wife, who had died. He thought again how strange it had seemed when he first learned that papa had been married to someone beside mamma.

In that first family there had been seven children, papa had said, but one had died when only a tiny baby, leaving six children for papa to take care of all alone.

Then came mamma's short list, for she had long ago told them that she had been a widow when she met the kind minister, Diettrich Neufeld, married him, and brought her two children to his home.

Papa and mamma's list of seven names was much the best, John always thought happily at this exact point, for he and Walter belonged among them. Through his closed eyelids he seemed to see the names as so often he had written them on his school tablet to show his playmates. Beside the name of each one still living at home in this big pinkish-colored farmhouse he marked an imaginary X.

PAPA'S LIST
1. Mary
2. Katie
3. Caroline
4. Jake
X 5. Nettie
6. Bertha

MAMMA'S LIST
X 1. Dave
X 2. Annie

PAPA *AND* MAMMA'S LIST
X 1. Linda
X 2. Walter
X 3. John
X 4. Wilfred
X 5. Sarah
X 6. Mildred
X 7. Rolland

The names wavered, blurred, and faded into nothingness until John felt Walter's sharp elbow jab against his back. He roused as his older brother flung back the warm woolen covers and shivered his way across the room's inky blackness.

"Wh—what? Is it Christmas morning?" John struggled drowsily to a half-sitting position in a vain attempt to see his brother.

"No, it isn't, but it ought to be," Walter whispered sharply. "I've been listening and listening for that crazy old clock to strike, but I haven't heard a sound. I just know papa forgot to wind it, and it's run down. If it has, we won't know when to get up, because papa's watch is broken."

"Papa didn't forget!" John protested. "You know he never forgets to wind grandfather's clock. And I don't think you've been lying awake any more than I have. You're just imagining things."

"I'm not either! Why, I know I've been awake for hours. I'm going down right now and feel those clock hands to find out if it isn't time to get up and look at our Christmas presents. I can hardly wait to see if our trains are there."

John burrowed deep under the covers as he heard Walter tiptoe carefully down the narrow back stairs that led to the big clock in the main hallway. His sleepy lids fluttered open at the warning click that always sounded just before the chimes struck the hour but they had closed tight before Walter's hasty return.

"Bong-bong-bong-bong-bong-bong-bong!" The sound jerked John upright beside loud-snoring Walter just as he heard papa's voice calling from the stair door.

"Nettie — Dave — Annie — Linda — Walter — John — Wilfred — Sarah! Merry Christmas! It's time to get up! I've already let you sleep an extra hour this morning. Hurry now!"

John shivered as the chill air crept across his shoulders. He flinched as it burrowed stealthily under his gray woolen underwear and crawled down his shrinking back. For the hundredth time he heartily wished that he were either as old as Mary, Katie, Caroline, Jake, or Bertha, who were

11

away from the farm, or as young as Mildred and Rolland, who were still too little to be much help in the breakfast preparations or the barnyard chores.

"I wonder why it's so pitch dark outside," papa remarked as the boys sleepily stumbled along the snowy path to the big unpainted barn. "Of course, it's always dark on winter mornings in Canada, but it seems even darker than usual today."

John peered up at the blue-black sky, made ghostlier still by small white clouds scudding past the moon's pale light. He thought longingly of mamma's cozy kitchen and those mysterious humps and bumps under their long, sheet-covered breakfast table. He determined to hurry as fast as he could with his milking so that he would be one of the very first to sit down at that table and see his presents. John knew that he and Walter would be the happiest boys in Saskatchewan if only they found their eagerly longed-for wind-up trains beside their breakfast plates.

"I hope it isn't clouding up for a blizzard. Cousin Dave's bringing Caroline and the children over for Christmas dinner. They can't get here if it storms too hard," papa continued, wiping the frost rime from his drooping mustache and beard.

John and Walter thought that they didn't care how much it stormed if they could only finish their chores quickly and hurry back into the warm farmhouse. In the hay-scented, lantern-lighted barn they milked as fast as they could, sitting close to the gentle-eyed cows and leaning their foreheads against the animals' warm flanks. "There, I'm done," said

12

John happily, rising quickly from his three-legged milking stool and giving old Rosie a pat.

"So'm I!" Walter added, picking up his heavy bucket. "Come on. Let's go!"

Quickly they carried their pails of rich foaming milk up to the big icy pantry, where after breakfast mamma and the girls would strain it through snowy-white cloths into shining tin milk pans.

Then they rushed to the wash bench in the big kitchen. While Walter carefully poured a stream of hot water into the granite washpan, John ladled an equal amount of cold water out of the nearby water bucket. As they washed their hands in the homemade soap's sudsy lather, they sniffed hungrily of mamma's good cooking: creamy oatmeal porridge, rye toast oozing yellow butter, poached eggs nestled close together in a deep bed of crisply browned potatoes, and cups of steaming Prips, a cereal drink homemade from ground wheat, barley, and molasses. Walter and John ravenously eyed the extra treat of holiday peppernuts—mamma's rich biscuit dough well-seasoned with spices—just the right size for "dunking" in their hot drink.

"Um-m-m! That looks good," sighed John, gazing longingly at the food-laden stovetop and warming oven. He gave his still-damp hands a hasty second drying on the back of his patched overalls and then slid into his place on the long bench just behind two-years-older Walter and just ahead of two--years-younger Wilfred.

"Wait a minute, please, everybody," mamma reminded cheerfully, her plump cheeks flushed red from the cookstove's fiery heat. "As soon as papa says grace, Nettie and Annie will lift off the cloth so that you can see your presents. Then we'll eat breakfast. It'll keep hot on the stove until we're ready."

"Komm, Herr Jesu,
Sie unser Gast;
Segne was du uns
In Gnade bescheret hast,
Wir bitten dich
In Jesu Name. Amen."

(Come, Lord Jesus,
Be our guest;
Bless what Thou hast
In grace showered upon us,
We implore Thee
In Jesus' name. Amen.)

John and Walter bent their heads and wriggled uneasily on the hard bench as papa's deep voice rumbled on in the old familiar grace. They scarcely dared look up, even after he had finished and the girls had carefully lifted the long muslin table covering from the eagerly anticipated presents.

"There, children," papa and mamma cried together. "Merry Christmas to you!"

"Merry Christmas! Merry, merry Christmas!" cried everyone at once, while John and Walter blinked their eyes and stared unbelievingly at the long table in front of them. Quickly they saw that each breakfast plate held just the same small gifts that had been theirs for as long as they could remember: one orange and two Jonathan apples apiece for a special treat, a big handful of small hard satin candies with their beautifully colored designs of flowers and stripes, and another handful of peanuts and walnuts. John and Walter remembered other years when they had received jack-knives in addition to those goodies.

But this Christmas—oh, this wonderful, wonderful Christmas! They reached out and grabbed each other for sheer joy as their dazzled eyes stared straight at two little wind-up trains. There they sat: each tiny engine with three cars trailing behind it—a coal car, a tank car, and a red caboose. In the soft glow of the Aladdin lamp in the exact center of the table the colors on the small trains gleamed richly.

"Our trains! Our wind-up trains! We've got them! Thank you, Mamma! Thank you, Papa! They're—they're wonderful," they said over and over again.

Never had the boys seen such wonderful gifts. Their joyful shouts rose to the rafters and mingled with the excited thanks from the other family members: the older girls, happy over the new clothing piled neatly on the floor at their appointed places; the older boys with their warm coats; the younger girls with their dolls and the baby with his wooden spool rattle. Hours flew by like minutes while the boys' tiny trains sped round and round their little tracks, and the girls' dolls became suddenly ill and recovered with the expert nursing care of their young mothers, who frowned at the boys' noisy play.

"I thought the folks were going to stop at noon on their way over to Uncle Jake's," John said to mamma as she bustled back and forth, stuffing a fat goose in readiness for the hot oven. "We wanted to show our cousins our new trains."

"Well, I thought they'd be here too," mamma answered, shutting the heavy oven door with a clang. "I can't understand why they drove up here at three o'clock in the afternoon and then went right on. I'd asked them to have a bite with us at twelve noon, but I couldn't stop in midafternoon to visit. Caroline and Dave and the children'll be here around six o'clock to eat Christmas dinner and spend the night with us. They're going to stop at grandpa and grandma's on the way, so they may be a little late; but I'll have dinner ready on time so that we can sit right down when they do get here!" John heard her sigh as she looked out the window.

"I hope we aren't going to have a storm. It stayed dark so late this morning and now, when it should be getting dark, it's still light. It reminds me of the famous Dark Day in history, when everything was turned topsy-turvy and the chickens went to roost in the daytime."

"That was May 19, 1780, Mamma. We read about it in school," John ventured, proud at this chance to quote an important historical fact.

"Well, whatever this day proves to be, you boys'd better get the cows milked and the horses fed and watered a little early tonight so you'll be all cleaned up for Christmas dinner and visiting afterward. The girls' beaus are coming over to spend the evening too; and I want you to look neat and clean and be on your best behavior while they're here."

John, Walter, Dave, and Wilfred grinned at one another as they put on their sheepskin jackets and warm knitted mittens and hurried down the well-worn path to the barn.

"Looks like they'd all get here in plenty of time for a long evening, so the girls should be real happy," John added. Dusk comes early on the wintry Canadian plains, but today at five o'clock John saw that it was as light as the noon hour. "Let's hurry up and finish the chores. I can smell that roast goose and dressing clear down here."

How good mamma's cooking tasted to the ten hungry young folks and two adults who finally sat down to their Christmas feast after a vain wait for their guests.

"It's a shame Dave and the folks couldn't get here!" papa exclaimed, looking at the delicately browned fowl, the fluffy mashed potatoes and thick gravy, the many side dishes of peas, beans, corn, dressing, pickles, jellies, zwieback, and the mince pie and plumimousse dessert served with accompanying cups of smoking-hot Prips.

"Yes, it's a shame they're not here," said mamma, after the dinner work was done and the last dish was put away in the pantry cupboard. "But, as I told the boys, it's been a queer sort of day all along. First of all, it stayed dark late this morning and now, although our old clock says past six, it's as light outside as midday. Then the folks didn't stop by until almost three, and Caroline and Dave didn't come at all. I declare—it's really been a topsy-turvy Christmas, for a fact."

"I don't care how topsy-turvy it's been, do you? It's been the best Christmas I ever had in my whole life. Just think. We got our wind-up trains. I'd have felt topsy-turvy for sure if we'd missed getting these," John whispered to Walter as they both reached for their precious gifts.

"Yes, you're right, Mamma," they heard papa's deep voice agreeing. "I can't understand why the folks haven't come. I guess that maybe the children are sick."

"John, I wish you'd look out and see if any of the folks are on the way now," mamma said. "Seems to me I hear sleigh bells. Look down the lane; it's still light enough so that you can see clear to the bend in the road."

Obediently John hurried to the tall narrow kitchen window, pushed aside the starched white curtain, and strained his eyes down the snowy lane. But, though he stared as hard as he could, he saw no familiar bobsled in sight. Slowly he shook his head.

"I don't see one single person coming down the road, Mamma, not even the girls' beaus, Jake and Nick," he said, turning back toward the family.

"Well, we'll begin our games the same as we do on Tuesday Home Party nights," mamma said cheerfully. "Perhaps all of them will come yet, and if they do, we've certainly got enough food to feed everybody."

Everyone took part in the games and ate their Christmas apples and candies; the younger children with real enthusiasm, the older girls with but halfhearted interest. John saw their eyes wander eagerly toward the kitchen window and their bright glances dull as the old timepiece ticked on and on.

As the clock chimed the hour, John and Walter chanted, "Seven, eight, nine." They sent their little trains on a last journey around the three-foot track as they heard papa's warning call.

"Time for bed, everybody! I've let you children stay up an hour later than usual; I kept thinking our folks and friends would surely come. I declare. I've a good notion to saddle up Jack and ride that twelve miles over to Dave's. Something out of the ordinary must've happened, or they'd have been here. They're as regular as clockwork in everything they do." Then the boys saw his bright eyes twinkle merrily as he smiled at mamma.

"You were right, Mamma, when you said it was a topsy-turvy Christmas Day. The folks missed getting here for the noon meal. Dave and Caroline missed eating Christmas dinner with us, and the girls missed sitting in the parlor with their beaus.

"Now we'd better get to bed so we won't miss out on our sleep. Up the stairs, all of you!"

John's feet felt so heavy they fairly dragged. Close behind Walter and Dave and ahead of Wilfred, he clumped up the winding stairway toward their bedroom, clutching his precious little metal train. He hated to put it down even for the minute or two necessary to slither out of his outer clothing and pull off his high laced shoes and woolen socks.

"It's certainly been a grand Christmas," he said, "even if the folks didn't come."

19

"Well, I'll like next Christmas better, 'cause then maybe I'll get *my* train," wistfully added little Wilfred.

"Sh!! Be quiet. Somebody's downstairs talking to papa!" warned Dave.

"Who in the world could be here at this time of night?" John asked.

"I don't know, but I'm going to find out," whispered Walter. "Come on, you fellows. Let's look down our secret peek hole and see what's going on."

Flat on their stomachs, the four boys lay on the cold floor and peered curiously down the small opening.

"Are you sick?" they heard Caroline's husband Dave ask anxiously at the open door, looking in surprise at papa's baggy nightshirt.

"Sick? Of course I'm not sick! Whatever gave you that idea?" The listening boys heard papa's quick answer. "Come in out of the cold. We'd decided that you or the children were under the weather. What happened?"

"What happened? Why, nothing happened. Never felt better in my life," they heard Dave's reply. "But you can't blame me for thinking a man's sick who'll invite his folks for Christmas dinner and then go to bed before they get there. 'Course, we're a mite late, but it's not more than six-thirty right now. When we found the house all dark I decided to drive on, but Caroline was so worried she made me come to the door to see what was wrong."

"*Six-thirty!* Did you say it was only six-thirty?" papa's reply thundered up the small ventilator.

20

"Why, our old clock just struck the half hour, but it struck *nine*-thirty—NOT *six*-thirty. We waited until nine for you, and then we went to bed."

"Nine-thirty!" exclaimed Dave in amazement. They heard him snap open his heavy gold watch and saw his hand hold it out toward papa.

"See for yourself, man. See for yourself. Doesn't that say six-thirty as plain as the nose on your face?"

Quietly, ever so quietly, the brothers inched away from the floor opening and tiptoed breathlessly across the creaky floor. They scarcely dared breathe until they had let themselves down into their beds and pulled the warm covers snugly around them.

"What in the world happened?" John whispered anxiously. "Are we *all* crazy, or is it only Dave?"

John felt the bed shake and heard Walter choke with stifled laughter before he answered. "No one's crazy. But I guess I'm to blame. You see, when I got up to feel the clock this morning, I must have shoved those old hands around a couple of hours. No wonder this has been a topsy-turvy day. We've been three hours ahead of everyone else all day long!"

"O Walter!" John gasped.

"Well, papa was right, after all," Walter said. "The rest of the family missed out on all their plans and our guests missed their Christmas dinner. Now be quiet and don't let him hear us talking about what really happened. I want to miss out on that licking he'd give me if he knew I was to blame for the queerest topsy-turviest Canadian Christmas we've ever had."

21

Chapter 2
Horse in a Cradle

WHY don't you slowpokes hurry up? You know you've got chores to do as soon as you get home. Can't you go any faster than that?" Dave grinned teasingly as he pedaled rapidly past his trudging brothers.

"Oh! I wish I had a bike! I'd show him a thing or two. I'd give just about anything for a bike. Wouldn't you, Walter?" John questioned as the boys kicked and scuffed their way along the snowy school path. His mouth drooped downward, and his merry brown eyes lost their twinkle as he watched his older half-brother, Dave, steer his rickety wheel round the icy bend in the road.

"Sure, I'd like one, all right," Walter sighed gustily. "But you know as well as I do there's no chance of papa's buying a bicycle for us. He's got all he can do just providing for our big family. And it takes every cent that he earns from his work as a minister and from our farm even to do that!"

"When we're older maybe we'll have saved up enough money to buy Dave's bike, if it holds together that long," John hopefully suggested. "Or maybe we could get jobs somewhere and earn enough to buy a new one."

Horse in a Cradle

"How?" Walter scoffed. "Do you really think we'll save much from the eighty cents spending money we earn each year from our gardens? And as for getting a job—well, that plan's no good, and you know it. We couldn't get full-time jobs unless we dropped out of school and papa and mamma wouldn't let us do that. They both think that education's too important!

"Besides, Dave wouldn't part with his precious bike even if we had the money to pay for it. I don't think he'd give up that bicycle for anything."

"Oh, yes, he would," assured John. "I know one thing that'd make him trade his bicycle to us."

"What?" questioned Walter.

"Why, he'd give it up in a minute if he had a horse. He even said so a while back. Don't you remember one night at the supper table when we were all talking about horses?

"He said, 'Well, when I get a horse to ride, you boys can have my old bicycle. I'll be through with it for good by that time.'"

"Yes, and 'if wishes were horses, even beggars would ride,' mamma said. I remember that too," Walter added sourly. "You must be crazy in the head if you don't know that a horse costs ten times as much as that old bike."

"Sure, a new one would. But an old horse wouldn't cost as much as an old bike," John added quickly, his eyes once again brightly alert. "Walter, I've got a good idea!"

"What?" grunted doubtful Walter.

"Why, I'm going by Uncle Jake's place and talk to him. It's only a half mile over there. He said

23

They Rubbed Old Bill With Kerosene and Fed and Watered Him
Until Papa Had to Warn Them

something to papa about Old Bill just last week. Come on. Maybe we can make a deal with him."

John broke into a jog trot, the buckles on his knee breeches flashing in the cold sunlight as his legs pumped up and down.

Walter followed reluctantly, but John saw that his brother's expression had changed considerably by the time he entered Uncle Jake's big barn and heard their uncle's reply to John's question.

"Now, there's the critter I told you about. He isn't much to look at, but he isn't so very old either. Maybe four or five years. However, he's a real good-dispositioned nag and one you'd have no trouble with at all.

"Main difficulty is he's so thin and poor right now that he's gotten clear down in his stall, and I ain't figured on no way to get him out without shooting him. If you two young ones can do anything with him, you can have him free and welcome. He's no good to me; that's sure and certain."

John and Walter stared at each other, wide-eyed and breathless. "A horse," their eyes said. "A horse of our very own!"

"You really mean that we can have him?" John questioned unbelievingly.

"Sure I mean it," Uncle Jake nodded. "But it'll be your problem to get him out of here. Seeing as how he can't get up, he isn't able to walk over to your barn. So you boys'll have to figure out just how to get him over there. I'm too busy to bother with the critter. You boys talk it over and do whatever you want to while I go ahead and finish up my chores."

Quickly John and Walter tiptoed up to the horse and stood staring down, even now scarcely believing their good luck.

"Well! What a horse!" John and Walter jumped as they heard Dave's voice directly behind them.

"When did you come in? I didn't hear you!" Walter gasped.

"Just now—just when Uncle Jake said you could have that old nag if you'd drag him out of here. What makes you think you want anything as moth-eaten as that? Why, he's even got lice all over him, and he's too weak to stand up."

Words fairly poured forth as John and Walter both tried at once to convince Dave that this was the horse for him—that on this very horse he could ride gaily ahead of them while they took turns pedaling the bicycle behind Old Bill's heels.

"You'd like to have a horse, wouldn't you, Dave?" John asked as they breathlessly concluded their sales talk.

"Sure, I'd like one, but I don't know about him," Dave said, glancing scornfully at the gaunt creature stretched weakly on the barn floor. "Why, about all you can say in his favor is that he's still breathing! But come on. We'll go home and hitch up Dolly to the stoneboat. When we bring it back I'll help you load Old Bill on the sled and take him to our barn. But from then on it'll be strictly up to you boys. If he turns out all right, I'll trade you my bike for him. If he doesn't—well, I'll still have my bike to ride."

Soon the old barn was filled with shrill cries of "Pull harder! Over this way. Careful now. Easy," as

26

the three boys pulled and rugged on poor Old Bill's legs and tail until they dragged him limply onto the stoneboat, a low sled made of two runners covered with rough planks.

The three boys were so hot and breathless when they finished their self-appointed task that the swirling snowflakes and freezing wind felt good against their flushed cheeks.

"There you are!" panted John as the three brothers stood back and looked at Old Bill sprawled helplessly on the clean straw at their feet. "We're here and so's Bill."

"Yep! Bill's here, but that's about all you can say for him. What'll you do with him now that he *is* here? Why, he can't even stand."

"I've got an idea!" John exclaimed. His eyes shone with excitement as he looked at Dave. "I know exactly what we can do if you'll help us, Dave.

"I think we could rig up a canvas sling that'd fit under that horse's belly and hold him up until his legs are strong enough to stand alone. Then we can begin right away to fatten him on oats and bundles (green feed). If we do that, it shouldn't be very long until he's well."

"Right now I'd say it'd be a long time before that bag of bones could do anything but rattle around in a canvas sling, but I'm willing to try your plan," Dave said. "And I'll help you rig up a block and tackle for holding old Bill up in the canvas sling."

It was dark before the homemade cradle was securely fastened, the patient horse hanging limply from its tight folds while he nibbled greedily at the oats held in Walter's outstretched hands.

"There. That's done!" Dave announced briskly. "Now tomorrow you boys had better get some kerosene and rub it on Old Bill. It's the best thing you can use to kill the lice that are swarming all over him."

John and Walter realized afterward that the next few days must have been trying ones to Old Bill, for in their eagerness to make the horse well they rubbed him with so much kerosene that they removed not only the lice but also great patches of skin and hair. And they fed and watered him so much and so frequently that papa had to warn them.

"You'll have a first-class case of bloat on your hands if you don't watch out," papa cautioned one evening as he followed them to the barn. "After all, you can't fatten a starved animal overnight. It'll take time. Three times a day is enough to feed and water him."

"But just look here, Papa," John called joyfully. "Old Bill's really lots better now. See? He can almost stand up alone. And his ribs don't stick out nearly so far as they did. Do they, Papa?"

The boys watched breathlessly as papa slid a practiced hand along the horse's back and legs, and eyed the coat that was beginning to have a faintly glossy sheen.

"He is better, isn't he?" Walter burst forth impatiently. "He's really going to get well now, don't you think, Papa?"

John and Walter felt like jumping for joy when papa finally nodded his head slowly up and down.

"Yes, boys. You've done a good job. I'd say that Old Bill's really going to get well and strong."

"Hooray! Hooray!" yelled the boys, startling Old Bill until he nearly jumped out of his swinging cradle. "Hooray for Old Bill."

Two months from the day that they had dragged the limp horse homeward on the stoneboat, John and Walter proudly rode their rickety bicycle down the snow-packed road close behind Old Bill. While Walter pedaled the bike John sat on the handle bars, and both of them called out to Dave, astride the plodding horse just ahead of their wobbling front wheel.

"Move along. Don't you know you've got chores to do?"

"Hurry up, you slowpoke."

"Can't you go any faster than that?"

The boys grinned as Dave half turned in his worn saddle. "Sure I can," he yelled back, slapping the reins against Old Bill's neck. "Just watch us. I'll show you who's a good rider. Here we go. Now try to catch us at the bend in the road!"

As Old Bill's flying hoofs pounded on the packed roadway, Walter pedaled faster and faster, trying in vain to close the widening gap between the creaking bicycle and the galloping horse.

John heard Walter's breath whistle in his throat as he strained against the pedals in a vain effort to catch the horseman now far ahead of them. He felt the treacherous sliding of the worn tires on the icy road. He saw disaster looming closer, ever closer to all of them.

"Hey! Watch out, Walter. The front wheel's wobbling. You're never going to make that turn. Neither is Dave. Old Bill's stumbling!

"Look out. We're heading for that big snow bank. We're—awk!—ugh!"

Three white figures rose slowly from the midst of a huge roadside snowdrift and stared silently at one another.

"Well," finally said shivering Walter as his cold fingers dug out the caked snow from his mouth and eyes and ears, "we've got our bike at last. But somehow I'm beginning to wonder just who got the best of this bargain after all."

Dave grinned sheepishly as he too raked snow from under his coat collar.

"I'm not sure just who did," he said. "You've got my bike, and I've got your horse in a cradle. But it seems almost as though you boys got the best of the bargain after all. It looks as though what I need is a cradle on the horse, so I can stay on!"

Chapter 3
Stuck-in-the-Mud

H URRY, boys! The girls are all ready to start the washing. Dave, will you please carry the buckets of hot water out to the washer while John and Walter bring Jack from the barn and hitch him up to our horse-driven washing machine? My, but I'm glad it's warm, sunny weather and we can wash the clothing out of doors. It saves so much disorder in the house."

"Well, mamma isn't the only one who's glad it's summer," added John as he and his brother ran down the path toward the big unpainted barn. "If it were winter, you and I'd be stuck in a hot, steamy kitchen all day, turning that old washing machine crank until our arms were ready to break off."

"I know it!" Walter agreed. "Why, mamma makes us turn that crank one hundred times for each tubful of clothes. And we always have nine tubfuls to wash, and each of those nine tubfuls has to be rinsed two times! Twenty-seven tubs of clothes to wash by hand. Think of it!

"I figured out that twenty-seven times one hundred is—let's see—that'd be two thousand seven

31

"Here I Go. Good-by, Old Stick-In-The-Mud"

hundred times we'd have to turn that crank. It makes my back ache even to think about it. I hope summer lasts forever."

Just as the boys harnessed Jack to the shaft that turned the washing machine, they saw Dave carefully pour the last bucketful of steaming hot suds into the battered wooden washing machine sitting under the shady poplar tree. Without further signal the faithful horse started on his monotonous day-long journey, round and round the never-ending circle worn in the grass by his patient hoofs.

Slosh-slosh-slosh! Creamy suds slapped against the sides of the washer. John and Walter watched gleefully as the suds frothed higher and higher until the topmost layer of rainbow-tinted bubbles broke off and floated to the ground.

"There. The machine's working all right and the girls can tend to the clothes. Now let's blindfold Jack, so he'll think we're still here," John proposed. "Hand me that sweater, will you? I'll tie it around his eyes, and he'll just keep right on going. Looky! See how he makes the circle? He even knows exactly where to lift up his feet and step over the drive-shaft. I'm sure glad we've got a horse who can work blindfolded."

"Let's go swing until it's time for the girls to put in the next batch of clothes. Come on, slowpoke; I'll 'pump' up the swing the first time."

The boys felt a goose-pimply thrill as they swung up, up, up in the big thirty-foot-high double swing that papa had fastened securely to heavy posts. They could scarcely bear to leave it long enough

33

to stop Jack and add more hot water to the tub or empty it entirely and refill with cold clean rinse water from the pump in the middle of the yard.

"Yoo-hoo. Walter! John! Our water barrels are almost empty. You'll have to harness up Jack and Dolly and take the wagon down to the lake. Don't play along the way. We need the water right now."

"Why can't mamma use our good well water for washing clothes?" grumbled John. He felt cross and ill used at having to leave the soaring swing.

"Because our well water's too 'hard' and it leaves rings around the tub and specks of red rust on the clothes," answered practical Walter. "You know that as well as I do, just as you know it's all right for drinking.

"Cheer up. We'll soon have the barrels full of 'soft' water from the lake, and then when we come back home we can play some more. Only this time let's get mamma's parlor sofa cushions and slide down the roof of the barn leanto. That's the most fun of all. Those pillows scoot along just like greased lightning."

"Not me," John answered. "I overheard her asking papa if he knew how in the world her good sofa pillows got so full of splinters. She said that the last time Annie's beau called on her he sat down on one and got right up in an awful hurry.

"I've been scared to death she'd ask me if we'd been playing with them and I'd have to tell her the truth. You know you can't fool mamma for very long. No, siree! Count me out on that idea. But I *am* going to take time for a quick dive and swim in the lake."

34

"No, you aren't," bossily contradicted Walter, slapping the reins on the horses' backs. "Papa said we'd better not swim until the lake got higher, and I know mamma wouldn't want you to, because we've got to hurry back, so the girls can finish the laundry. It's an all-day job even when things go right."

"Well, I don't care if it is. Girls shouldn't be so fussy and wear all those ruffled petticoats and doodads. They just get dirty and have to be washed every week. I'm not going to let them cheat me out of one dive anyway. Why, I'll be so steaming hot after filling all those big fifty-gallon barrels that I'll be ready to melt," snapped John. "And *I* think the water's high enough to swim in.

"If you want to be an old stick-in-the-mud and not go in, it's all right with me. But I just dare you to. I dare you—dare you—double dare you. So there."

As the team stood quietly in the four-foot depth at the edge of the little lake, the boys worked quickly, lowering, raising, and emptying the water buckets until all the barrels were brimful of cool, sparkling water. Then, true to his threat, John stripped off his shirt and overalls, and poised on the edge of the high wagon bed.

"Here I go. Good-by, old stick-in-the-mud!" he flung tauntingly over his bare shoulder just as he flashed out and straight down into the lake's blue water.

As Walter watched angrily, impatient to be on his way homeward, he determined to wait not one extra minute for John. He decided that as soon as his brother came to the surface, he'd demand that he climb back on the wagon and not take any more time that day for swimming.

"As soon as he came to the surface! As soon as he came to the surface!" the words rang like a bell in Walter's mind. He ran to the wagon's edge and peered anxiously downward, straining his eyes for a glimpse of his younger brother's sleek wet head.

"He's had time to swim way out under water. By this time he'd have to come up for air," he thought frantically. But although the frightened Walter stared straight down at the exact spot where John had vanished he could see nothing but spreading murky waves that clouded the clear water with a muddy tinge.

"He's caught. John's caught in the mud on the bottom of the lake!" Walter gasped. "That's what is wrong. Oh! What can I do? I don't think I'm strong enough to pull him out. But I've got to. I've got to save my brother!"

But even as agonizing doubts and fears ran through his mind, his trembling fingers jerked off his outer clothing, and his shaking legs carried him straight to the spot from which John had dived.

Walter drew a deep lung-filling breath as he flung himself outward. Then down, down into the inky darkness he pulled himself, swimming steadily toward the spot where he felt that John *must* be. But though his fingers touched bottom and explored as far as they could reach he felt nothing but the thick slimy mud that caught and held its victims.

36

"I'll have to go up. I've got to breathe!" he thought desperately. "I can't stay down here another second. Yet even as his tortured lungs demanded fresh, pure air his hands reached out in one last, desperate grasp for John.

"There. There's something—I felt something— near—if I can only reach—— It's John! He's head down in the mud. He must be smothered by now."

Walter felt a sudden, life-giving surge of strength through his tired body. Quickly he grabbed the helpless John and pulled, pulled, pulled until he felt his arm sockets almost give way. But still his brother's body held fast in its muddy lake-bottom trap.

"I won't give up," Walter moaned. "I can't leave him here." As he tugged once more with the last of his waning strength, his heart pounded until it threatened to burst his chest and his muscles tightened like whipcord.

"Pull! Pull!" he thought dizzily. "Pull hard."

Then, with a sudden rush, as though in answer to his anxious prayer, the two brothers rose quickly to the surface. Somehow Walter felt himself hanging onto the wagon while he slowly pushed and pulled the half-unconscious John into the wagon bed.

Long minutes passed before either boy could speak. Walter felt his breath rasp painfully in his throat while black specks swam strangely before his eyes. He saw that mud-covered John lay like a broken, chocolate-coated rag doll, arms and legs flung at odd angles.

Then, as John's hand moved weakly to wipe away the mud from his eyes and nose and mouth,

Walter sat up and reached for the last-filled bucket of clear, cold water.

"Here, I'll pour this over you. You can't see anything through all that dirt." Walter dragged the sloshing bucket to his brother's side, cupped his hands, and poured handful after handful of clean water over John's blackened face. No word was spoken until John had recovered enough to cleanse himself thoroughly in readiness for the homeward journey.

"What'll we tell mammal She'll be sure to ask us why we're so late," Walter questioned as the horses started slowly on the return toward the Neufeld farm.

"Well, we won't tell her any more than we have to, because then she'd worry about us every time we came here for water," John painfully replied through a throat that felt raw and sore. "But you know mamma. She'll guess what happened, sure as my name's John Orlando. No one can ever fool mamma. Her eyes just look right straight through a fellow.

"Anyway, I don't care if I do get punished for being late. I'm so happy to be alive that even a whipping'd feel good. When I dived down into that sticky mud I thought I was stuck there forever. It was awful. And if it hadn't been for you, Walter, I'd still be there. Only I wouldn't be worrying about getting out of the water. I'd be dead."

John flashed his brother a sheepishly admiring smile that wordlessly said the sincere thanks that he could not express.

38

"I'm sorry I made fun of you, Walter. I guess you were right not to take a silly dare. I've decided it's lots better to be a stick-in-the-mud safe in the wagon than it is to be a stuck-in-the-mud down at the bottom of the lake. Believe me, I'm never going to try anything like that again."

Chapter 4
Family Fun

CHILDREN, you'd better take another helping of porridge," urged mamma. "You'll all need plenty of good hot breakfast; there's a busy day ahead for each one of us."

John's heart sank as he thought of the mountains of work awaiting the Neufeld family as they harvested their own potato crop. Well he knew that all of them, except mamma and the very youngest children, would have to go out into the fields. There the boys would dig the potatoes while the girls filled the tin pails and then carried and emptied them into the wagon box. As soon as each wagonload was piled high it would be drawn by the patient horses to the side of the huge pinkish-colored farmhouse and emptied into the yawning cellar underneath.

John remembered each fall's harvesting and how he always looked forward to the sight of those bushels and bushels of red-skinned Early Rose potatoes stacked on the cellar's dirt floor close beside the smooth white-skinned potatoes from the south field. He liked to look at the piles of yellow carrots awaiting winter burial beneath their warm covering of sand, the crisp green cabbages, round golden pumpkins, and tapering brown-veined parsnips. He never tired of staring at the shelves where hundreds and hundreds of quarts of home-canned peas and beans jostled against tasty jars of hard-to-get apricots, peaches, wild strawberries, and chokeberries. His nostrils always twitched pleasurably at the cellar's good nose-tingling smell of dirt, root vegetables, straw, crocks of sauerkraut and spicy dill pickles, and well-filled apple barrels.

All that cold, autumn day the busy workers toiled, their hands chapped and rough from the dirt and near-freezing weather. A brief noon lunch hour flew by on wings. By late afternoon John and Walter were thankful to see the last of the potato crop harvested and safely stored in the near-to-bursting cellar.

"Hurrah! There's the supper bell!" yelled Walter. He gratefully straightened his cramped back, getting ready to run home.

"What's the matter with you now, Mr. Crazy-to-work?" teased John. "I thought you just couldn't wait to get out here and dig in the dirt all day, like a dog chasing a gopher. Don't tell me you want to quit!"

"Aw, be still!" Walter growled. "You know we had to finish this job today, and we did. Besides, have you forgotten that our cousins are coming over this evening to play games? I've been looking forward to that all day. "I'm sure glad mamma lets us have one evening for our Home Party night, aren't you? None of the other youngsters at school get to have any fun at home like we do."

41

"Of course they don't," readily agreed John. "But that's because they run around town nights and do just about as they please. Papa and mamma won't let us. That's why we get to have a Home Party once a week.

"What do you suppose we'll do tonight?" he continued, brightening at the happy prospect of an evening of fun.

"Oh, we'll probably play some of the same old games—blindman's buff, I spy, and button-button—but I never get tired of them. And we can watch Nellie and Annie while they sit there like silly geese and make eyes at their beaus," added Walter.

"Say, that reminds me. I heard the girls talking about what they're going to wear and how they're going to frizzle up their hair in front and braid it in the back. It makes a fellow tired to listen to them talk. I suppose they'll beg mamma to let them light a fire in the coal stove in the parlor, so they can sit in there all evening instead of in the kitchen with us!"

"Well, I only hope I don't have to polish that stove again just so Nettie and Annie can put on their stylish airs," John groaned. His arms ached as he recalled the effort he had put forth on previous rubbings and polishings to brighten the huge six-foot-high heating stove with its lion-head decorations on each corner.

"Seems to me they could sit in the kitchen. It's plenty good enough for me!" John repeated. He thought lovingly of mamma's big spicy-smelling kitchen, with the cookstove's red eyelets winking a cheerful welcome across the hand-braided rug and the long table set with tasty, steaming food.

He and Walter hurried even faster, so that they were quite out of breath when they finished a quick scrubbing in the granite washpan and sat down to mamma's good meal of bean soup richly sprinkled with potatoes and onions, boiled eggs, and home-made light bread and butter, with a choice of jelly or syrup for dessert. As usual, John could scarcely make up his mind which one of the two he really wanted. First he chose mamma's quivering ruby-red jelly, only to decide on the rich golden-brown syrup, for well he knew that mamma wouldn't let him have both. He silently vowed, as he always did at this point, that when he grew up and married he would have *both* jelly and syrup every day.

As soon as papa had finished the blessing they began eating rapidly and silently, until hunger's keen edge was filed from healthy appetites. Pitchers of milk and plates of crusty bread were emptied and refilled, emptied and refilled. Finally John nudged Walter.

"Say, how many eggs has Dave eaten tonight?" he whispered.

"I don't know, but I'm on my fifth, and he got a head start," Walter softly replied. "Just watch him, will you? Whenever the plate's passed to him he turns it around so he always gets the biggest egg. Isn't he piggish? Somehow he always manages to get the biggest serving!"

"It isn't fair," stormily whispered John. "I wish I was older so I could act like Dave and not get scolded any more than he does."

"Much good being older'd do you," scoffed Walter. "I'm older than you, but I don't get to grab the biggest serving of everything, do I? Anyway, I remember once when Dave got what was coming to him. That was the time he took the biggest Easter egg on the dish."

The boys choked with laughter over the remembrance of Dave as he had picked up his steel knife and hit the egg a quick crack.

The egg had spouted with a "Whi-i-sh!"

"Look out!" Annie and Nettie had cried, jumping up from the table.

"It's all over you, Dave," little Sarah had screamed "on your face and everywhere."

"It's a raw egg," had shrieked tiny Mildred, "an' it's even up in your hair."

"Mam-ma!" frightened baby Rolland had bawled loudly.

"Here, here, boys," John and Walter heard mamma speak quickly. "Stop your giggling at the supper table. Everyone be quiet, please. I can't hear myself think when there's so much noise, and I've something nice to tell you.

"Since you've all had a hard day's work I thought I'd make one of our extra special desserts for Home Party night," mamma said. "Bring on the cream puffs, please, Nettie, and start them at papa's place."

"Um-m," sighed the children rapturously.

"Cream puffs. Oh, goody!" squealed Mildred, bouncing up and down on the hard bench. "I just love your cream puffs, Mamma."

"Who doesn't?" said Dave. He greedily eyed the big platter of cream-filled puffs.

John and Walter saw that already their brother had picked out the largest serving of all. But they couldn't believe their eyes when they saw Nettie carefully saving back that particular cream puff for Dave.

"Oh-h-h!" Cries of joy rose as the blue platter made the rounds and the youngsters lifted off the crisp pastries and bit into their sweet, melting softness.

As John and Walter waited hungrily, they saw the platter stop in front of Dave. They watched as his hand quickly darted out, over, and across to the outer edge, where it grabbed the very grandfather of all cream puffs. They watched as he opened his mouth wide and sank his white teeth deep into the exact top of the delicious flaky pastry.

"Wh—ugh! What on earth's in that old cream puff?" he stammered. "I—it—it sets my teeth on edge. Ugh! It tastes simply awful!"

"Dave! Dave! Will you never learn your lesson?" cried mamma, laughing so hard that her cheeks flamed crimson. And as the family watched greedy Dave pick the now-wadded bits of cotton out of his teeth, they too began to laugh with her. The boys saw that even papa shook so helplessly with mirth that he had to give his beard an extra wiping to clean off the little blobs of whipped cream he spilled.

But at last the supper table was cleared and the dishes done just in time to admit the cousins to a neat, shining kitchen. The girls scarcely had

He Glanced Over His Shoulder as He Sidled
Toward the Large Family of Paper Dolls

time to finish primping before their beaus arrived, and John found, to his deep disgust, that his worst fears were realized. He had to build a big fire in the tall parlor stove!

Mamma passed the plate of rosy apples and the deep dish of dried sunflower seeds while gay laughter and happy voices rang out in talk and songs and well-loved games. John and Walter joined in the games until they spied Sarah and Mildred sitting in a corner, making their own paper dolls from the T. Eaton Mail Order Company catalog.

"Look at those silly girls!" scoffed John. "Cutting out more paper dolls. Why, the house's littered with them now. Say, I've got a good idea. Come on; let's tease them, just for fun."

"How?" questioned Walter. "I don't know what you can do. Mamma'll punish you if you grab them or twist their arms or anything really mean!"

"Oh! I won't hurt *them!*" John sturdily answered. "I'll just fix those dolls so they'll never be any good again. Come on. If you'll call Sarah and Mildred over by you and talk to them, I'll show you what I'm going to do."

John waited only long enough to see his younger sisters hurry across the big kitchen in response to Walter's call.

"Now for the butcher knife!" he thought, grabbing mamma's sharpest bone-handled carving knife from the kitchen drawer. He glanced over his shoulder as he sidled toward the large family of dolls neatly ranged on the spotless linoleum-covered floor.

"Good! Walter's still talking to the girls. Here goes." John slashed quickly across one paper doll after another until more than a dozen paper men, women, and children lay neatly guillotined.

"Now for the rest of them," he thought. But even as he reached for another victim Sarah saw the flashing knife.

"You stop that. Mamma! John's cutting up my best paper dolls!" she wailed, running toward him. "I'll grab your arm, you old meanie, and make you stop."

Just as John raised his arm for one more downward slash he saw Sarah spring toward him. He felt her arms grasp his wrist; he felt the razor-sharp knife swing in a half-circle. Then he felt a stinging pain and saw the bright red blood gushing from his half-severed thumb.

"My thumb's cut off!" John wailed, almost sick with shock and pain. "I'm bleeding to death."

"Mamma! Boohoo! John's bleeding to death!"

Mildred and Sarah began crying at the top of their lungs, while Walter drew his breath in a long whistle as he stared at his brother's wounded hand.

"Here, here, children, let me see!" John heard mamma's comforting voice over his shoulder and saw her kind eyes quickly sense the situation. Then, as everyone gathered around all at once, he shrinkingly realized that he was the center of attention.

"Well, Johnny, it's a bad cut all right, but I think I can bandage it so you won't lose your thumb," mamma said. "Annie, run and tear off some soft

48

linen rags and bring the carbolic salve; as soon as the bleeding stops I'll put on a poultice and get John to bed so he can be quiet."

John thought it seemed strangely nice to have mamma going upstairs with him to help him undress, just as she used to do when he was a little boy. He felt safe and secure as she put her warm arms around him to kiss him good night. And the painful throbbing in his half-severed thumb felt less unbearable as she knelt beside him and prayed her simple prayer for help and trust and forgiveness.

"Good night, my boy. Try to sleep as best you can. I know the wound's painful, but by tomorrow it will be more bearable. I'll come up again later on after our guests leave."

John bit his lips to keep back the tears that pressed against his burning eyelids, and drew in his breath against the pain that swept like liquid fire up his injured arm. Minutes dragged like hours as merry voices and laughter streamed upward through the stovepipe hole ventilator.

"Johnny," he heard a soft, tearful whisper from the dark doorway. He turned his aching head slowly on the pillow as he saw a small figure creep quietly to his bedside.

"John, I'm sorry I made you cut your hand," Sarah's voice sobbed. "O Johnny, I didn't mean to hurt you! I couldn't stay down there and play any more while you're sick up here."

John swallowed hard against the lump in his throat before he could speak, but his uninjured hand reached out and patted his little sister's shoulder.

Really-Truly Stories

"It's—Mamma said my thumb'll be all right. She said I'd always have a bad scar, but at least my thumb'll be there! I'm thankful for that!"

He felt his little sister's tears hot against his cheek as she snuggled close to him.

"Anyway, it served me right," he concluded. "It wasn't your fault at all, Sarah. If I hadn't been so selfish and mean, I wouldn't have got hurt.

"From now on I won't be so hateful and 'butt' into somebody else's business!" he ended. "Going to bed with a cut thumb isn't my idea of taking part in Home Party night."

Chapter 5
Too Many Sweet Maries

HURRY up, John. Mamma and papa want to see you. They said for you to come right away," Walter called. "Wilfred and I can finish the milking."

"What do they want?" John questioned anxiously. "Is mamma worse?"

"No, I don't think so, but she isn't any better either. The girls keep saying she's going to get well, but it doesn't look like it to me. I think they got a letter today from Uncle Frank; that's what they want to talk to you about. Why don't you go on up to the house? You'll never learn anything standing here."

John's heart sank as he ran up the muddy pathway. All mamma and papa's low-voiced conversations of many weeks past seemed to rush together into one loud shout: "You're going away. You're going away from Waldheim!"

A lump came into his throat. He swallowed hard as he stopped for a moment to stare at mamma's beloved garden, now spring-fresh and green in the sun's slanting rays. All at once he had the feeling that never again would he, as a boy at home, see mamma's feathery purple and white lilacs nodding their sweet-scented plumes up and down in a soft

51

Not Until John Was Finally Settled on One of the Hard Coach Seats
Did He Dare Draw a Long Breath. Then in Sheer Relief
He Decided on a Daring Plan

evening breeze. Never again would he see the tall evergreens reaching their tips prayerfully toward the blue Canadian sky. All at once the landscape blurred; he hastily wiped his wet eyes before he turned and hurried toward the kitchen door.

He was almost breathless by the time he reached his mother's room and sank down into a chair by her bed. "What is it, Mamma?" he choked, coughing a little to clear the aching feeling from his throat. "I was worried when Walter said you'd sent for me."

"You're a good boy, John," he heard papa say soberly. "Now there's nothing to get excited over as far as mamma's concerned. She's no better and no worse than she has been for months.

"No, what mamma and I want to talk about is Uncle Frank's letter. It came this afternoon; we'll have to decide right away what we're going to do. Your Uncle Frank needs someone to help with the plowing, and since he knows we need the money he's offered the job to you for fifty dollars a month. That's a man's wage, son. You've worked on the farm ever since you were five or six. You ought to be able to handle the plowing all right by now. What do you say?"

Fifty dollars! John thought. Why, fifty dollars was a fortune. He knew how many supplies were needed by the big Neufeld family and how pitifully few were the dollars that came in. He knew too that he was more than willing to help in any way he could.

But even as he nodded he wondered whether he'd ever be able to finish a school term without missing half the required time. It seemed to him that every spring and fall, as far back as he could remember, he had missed the May and June classes at the end of school and the September and October classes at the beginning of school. "Of course, papa, I'll go, and I'll bring all my wages home when I come," he said slowly. "Only—well, I'm wondering if I'll miss very much school next fall. I want to be able to go on to academy, but if I don't finish the eighth grade, I can't go. Will I be able to come back here by the time school starts again?"

John saw papa and mamma look hastily at each other. He heard papa clear his throat before he began talking. But even before his father started to speak, John knew what he was going to say. All the scrambled fragments of sentences barely overheard for months past fell into place like a puzzle now complete. Through a strange roaring in his ears he half heard papa's explanation.

"Hate to ask you to leave, but we need the money.... We've had to let this old place go....New home at Swift Current.... Come there next November.... We're sure you'll like our new place.... You can go to school there."

All during the long fifty-mile trip to Uncle Frank's, John huddled miserably in his seat, already homesick for the only home he had ever known. And John felt that Uncle Frank's opening remarks were not ones that would make any thirteen-year-old boy feel exactly able to do a man's work. He never forgot his uncle's first sentences.

"Hello there, John, glad to have you here. Hm-m! Seems to me you look pretty small for a thirteen-year-old. But I guess you can handle the farm work, or your father wouldn't have sent you.

"Now here's ten horses. Harness them up to that three-bottom plow. Put four horses in the lead and a row of six horses behind them. Then we'll chain the harrow and the packer on behind the plow.

"You'll have to watch out for that big gray stallion. He's real good-tempered most of the time, but when he's been shut up over the week end he's mighty frisky. Sometimes you'll have to give him his head and let him run once around the field.

"There! Now you can start. Come on, I'll show you where to begin plowing; then I'll go on with my own work. 'Every Man for Himself' is my motto."

John soon learned that Uncle Frank was right when he told him to be careful. And he was as careful as he knew how to be when harnessing the horses, especially the huge gray stallion, who towered high above him. But on this bright, sunny Monday he thought the horses seemed like naughty school children. Though he pulled with all his might, they kept going faster and faster.

"Slow down, there. Slow down," John called, tightening his grasp on the reins. "Whoa! I say. Whoa!"

P - i - n - g! John felt the seat shudder and quake as the plowshare struck solid rock beneath the rich topsoil. He felt the plow seat spring up like a diving board; he felt himself spinning out and up. T - h - u - d!

Then the ground was rising up to meet him. He felt a sickening crash. And then he knew only one thing—he had fallen in the midst of the moving

55

lines of horses. His heart pounded like a trip hammer as he rolled desperately to avoid the oncoming hoofs and the dreadful shining blades of the plow.

"Whoa!" he called thickly. But he was so out of breath that the word was no more than a faint croak.

"Whoa there! Whoa!" Despairingly he both prayed and yelled as he saw the cruel cutting blades come nearer and nearer. John thought that he would faint as the cold steel rasped against his bruised back. He moaned, closed his eyes, and waited for death.

Suddenly John heard only the quick, nostril-blown breathing of the horses and the jingling of their harness as they stood quietly switching their long tails. Unbelievingly he opened his eyes and stared up at the plow directly above him. He stared unbelievingly as he saw that he lay directly against the blades; the horses had stopped just in time!

Shakily he got to his feet and staggered away from the team. Suddenly he felt weak and ill. For a time he lay flat on the ground, drawing deep breaths of fresh air, telling himself over and over again that it was good to be alive.

Except for this one near-accident, John really enjoyed the summer. He felt that Aunt Nettie, papa's own sister, was like a mother to him. Not only did she see that he ate until he could eat no more, but she washed and ironed and mended his clothing. She looked out for him as carefully as she did for her own family.

And Uncle Frank was good too, in his way. John soon learned that he was expected to work hard, but he also learned that Uncle Frank treated him well and paid him fairly.

John thought that the best part of the whole summer season came at the very last. Then Uncle Frank actually paid him five dollars a day to haul water from the lake for the steam threshing machine. He often wondered whether he was honest in taking so much money for this work. The day began at 5 A.M., with breakfast at six o'clock, noon dinner at eleven, lunch brought out to the fields at four o'clock, and a huge supper served at eight in the evening. He was sorry when the two-week threshing season was over.

But at last John took out his battered old suitcase and watched Aunt Nettie neatly pack his scanty belongings: his extra pair of trousers, underwear, two shirts, socks, and pair of shoes.

"There, nephew!" she said briskly as she snapped shut the lid. "You're all ready to go. I've put up a box lunch for you, so that you can have some good home-cooked food on the way. You can spend some of your own money to get anything extra you want. But be careful. I don't trust this boughten food. It's apt to be tainted.

"Now run along. Your uncle's ready to take you to the station. He's got your wages all counted out for you in greenbacks. Take good care of it. Don't let a pickpocket walk away with your summer earnings."

As John sat alone in the station after his uncle had told him good-by he kept thinking of his aunt's words and of mamma's last letter now crackling in his inner coat pocket. He remembered that mamma also had warned him to beware of thieves. She had told him to trust no stranger and to watch his luggage every minute.

John hastily moved his shabby suitcase, his box lunch, and his own shabby self to a corner of the depot. There he huddled, like a rabbit in its burrow, until his train arrived. He was thankful to hear its huffing and puffing, for he felt that everyone in the station knew about the roll of bills that his clenched fist held in his pocket.

Not until he was finally settled on one of the hard coach seats did John dare draw a long breath. And then, in sheer relief, he decided upon a daring plan. Cautiously he drew out a dollar and stared at it as he boldly decided to spend it all for just one thing—twenty Sweet Maries. His mouth watered as he recalled the one taste he had ever had of the rich chocolate-and-nut candy bars. Though they cost but five cents each, there had been no five-cent pieces to spare in the Neufeld farmhouse.

But now, John thought, he would treat himself from his own money to as many of them as he could eat in the two-day journey ahead of him. John made up his mind to waste no money on food. He decided that he would buy only the candy bars. All the rest of the money he would give to papa and mamma as soon as he reached his new home in Swift Current.

John never forgot the delicious melting taste of that first Sweet Marie chocolate bar. He never forgot the second, third, fourth, fifth—and he never forgot the twentieth one either, for by that time, at the end of his journey, he was so tired of the once-prized Sweet Maries that he could scarcely bear to think of them.

"Oh, but I'm glad to be home," he said as his tired legs climbed the front steps beside papa's hurrying ones. He thought how wonderful it was to see mamma's smiling face in the doorway and to feel her warm arms welcoming him. He thought how good it was to see all his brothers and sisters crowded close around. He scarcely had time to greet all of them before Mildred grabbed him by the arm.

"Come on, John," she begged. "Hurry up and get washed. We've got the best supper. It's all ready for you, and we've got dessert too."

"Supper?" said John. His tongue felt thick and coated with a furry sweetness. "Supper? Why, I—I guess I'm not very hungry, Mildred."

"Not hungry?" shrilled six-year-old Rolland. "Well, you'd better be hungry. Mamma's going to let us have a special treat tonight, just because you're home. You'll never guess what it is, so I'll tell you. It's *Sweet Maries.*"

From his miserable position on the back porch John heard mamma ask, "Where's John? Isn't he ready to eat?" And then he heard Rolland's childish answer.

"I don't think so, Mamma. He's being awful sick out in the back yard. So please, can I have his Sweet Marie?"

"Children, Children," Said Pale, Smiling Mamma,
"Let Me Sit Down and Catch My Breath"

Chapter 6
Mamma's Hezekiah Prayer

JOHN and Walter looked eagerly down the road, straining their eyes for the first glimpse of papa's old model-T Ford.

"Don't you think they ought to be home by now?" John asked for the twentieth time. "I wonder why they're so slow. I can hardly wait to see mamma again."

"Me either," sighed Walter. "It seems ages since she went away just before Christmas. But I suppose it takes a long time for a person to get over an operation like hers."

"It'll be wonderful to have her here with us," John spoke soberly. "Home never seems the same without mamma. Even Jake said so, just before he left. And from him that's really a compliment, because he isn't any relation at all to our mother."

"Well, I guess none of us ever think about our families' being all mixed up together. Mamma's always treated us just alike; that's why we all love her so much," Walter said.

John was the first to see the old car far down the lane. And when papa's model-T chugged up to the front gate he and Walter were the first ones to be there to greet their parents. The others crowded close behind them as the Ford wheezed to a stop. Then a babel of voices arose.

"Welcome home, Mamma."

"Oh, but it's good to see you back here again. We've missed you dreadfully."

"Let me help you out of the car, Mamma."

"Mamma, give me a kiss."

"Children, children," said pale, smiling mamma, "let me sit down and catch my breath; then I'll look at each one of you. It seems such a long time since I last saw my family that we'll almost have to get acquainted all over again." Laughingly they lined up in front of her, taking their places according to age. Quickly she called out their names and pretended to see whether everyone was present.

Linda (19)

Walter (17)

John (15)

Wilfred (13)

Sarah (10)

Mildred (8)

Rolland (6)

John's heart leaped as he heard mamma's happy voice. His eyes looked straight into Walter's with the glad thought that mamma sounded just like her old self.

Now that mamma was home again, the days seemed to fly by John saw that the work was done more quickly and that the younger children worked and played with out the bickering that had filled the house while mamma had been away at the hospital. He saw papa's stooped shoulders straighten and heard his hearty laugh ring out more and more often.

John hoped with all his heart that his mother was getting well and strong, and for a time he saw that she seemed much better. But at last the family could not fail to notice that she grew thinner and paler daily, while her steps became slower and slower. Finally papa called them all together while mamma was lying down.

"Children, I'm going to take mamma to Moose Jaw Hospital," he announced. "She's not getting any better here, but perhaps the hospital doctors can do something for her. At any rate, we'll try them and see. Now mamma wants to talk to each one of you before she goes, and I want all of you to try to be brave and cheerful. Don't make it harder for her by crying and being sad. You'd better go in one at a time. It won't tire her so much that way."

John and Walter went into mamma's room hand in hand, and stood beside her bed. John felt hot tears sting his eyelids as he saw how she had shrunk from a big, rosy, laughing woman to a thin, pale shadow of her former self. But he saw too that the kind eyes and quick smile were mamma's and the loving whisper of a voice was mamma's too. Quickly they knelt by her bedside as she motioned to them.

"You must be good boys while I'm away," she said gently. "Help papa all that you can. Be kind to the younger children. Try to do well in school.

63

Above all, go ahead and get an education. You'll try, won't you, my boys?"

"Yes, mamma, we'll try," they promised, their throats thick with unshed tears.

"Be good, John. Be a good boy, Walter. With God's help I may be coming back again. God bless both of you."

They felt mamma's thin hands upon their heads. Then, with a last kiss, they stumbled from the room.

After mamma left the days seemed to slip back into their old dragging way. Everyone tried to do his best, but somehow nothing ran so smoothly as it had when mamma was in charge. Of course, John thought, they missed papa too. But he had been away so much during the years that they were more accustomed to his absence. But they couldn't forget that mamma wasn't there. John almost hated to come home from school, since she was no longer at the door to meet him.

Yet her letters were hopeful, and they helped immensely to cheer the lonely family impatiently awaiting her return to Swift Current. Finally the time grew less and less until at last mamma wrote that she would surely be home in two weeks. Then it was one week. At last John's letter came.

"Mamma says she'll be home next Monday," he read excitedly. "Just think, folks; mamma'll be home Monday. We'll have to work hard and get everything all ready for her."

Hurriedly the Neufelds began cleaning and polishing, washing and ironing, cooking and baking, as if in readiness for the arrival of a small army.

John and Walter ran errands without grumbling and helped in every way they could to brighten up the home and yard for mamma's return.

On Sunday the telephone message came. Linda answered the sharp ring while the boys' straining ears tried to listen also.

"That must be papa calling long distance. Can you hear what he's saying?" John whispered to Walter as Linda's voice shook and then stopped.

"No, I can't," Walter replied briefly. "But—I'm afraid—let's go and find out what he said."

But John and Walter did not need Linda's sobbing whisper, "She's gone, children; mamma's gone," to know the awful truth.

"Gone!" John exclaimed. "But, Linda, she can't be. She was getting better. Why, I just got her letter a day or so ago saying she'd be home this week. There must be some mistake. There must be."

Frantically he grasped Linda's arms as though he, single-handed, could change the sad message that she had given them. John's eyes filled with tears as she shook her head.

"No, boys, there isn't any mistake, but in one way you're right, John. Mamma *is* coming home. But she isn't coming here. Papa said her last wish was to be buried in Waldheim. He's taking her there for burial.

"We'll have to get a permit for our car, so Walter can drive us to our old home town. Papa can't afford the twenty-five dollars for a car license; he said to try to get a special car permit so that we can go to the funeral. We don't have enough money to buy train tickets for all of us."

John and Walter never forgot that dreadful trip over the rough country roads leading to Waldheim. There was almost no conversation, only occasional sobs from the heartbroken children. And there was constant car trouble to plague them, either from the overheated engine or from the worn tires. The boys expected a blowout at least every forty miles, nor were they wrong in their estimate. Tears and car trouble. Car trouble and tears. They felt that if they could only last through the next few dreary days, they could meet any sorrow that might come to them later in life. They felt that nothing could be worse than this.

And then it was all over—the trip, the funeral services, and the nightmare journey home. All of them seemed dazed. It was not until tired-looking, aging papa called them together to resume their regular worship period that they heard his account of mamma's last days. And, strangely, it comforted them. The aching loss was still there, but, as John said, "It seems more bearable somehow since papa's told us all about mamma's wishes." John and Walter never forgot papa's solemn voice or his comforting words as he talked to them about what he called "mamma's Hezekiah prayer." The family sat silent and awestruck while papa's voice told the story.

"You all know the Bible story of Hezekiah," he began. "You remember how he prayed to the Lord to lengthen his life for fifteen years, so that he could finish his work. Just as his prayer was granted, so was mamma's prayer granted.

"When you were born, John, mamma almost died. In fact, she was actually slipping away from us then. As I knelt by her bed she whispered to me to pray. She wanted me to pray to the Lord to spare her life so that she might live to bring you up into young manhood, John. She wanted to live to care for the other little children that we had, not only our own Linda and Walter, and her Dave and Annie, but my children as well. For you know that mamma always loved all of you just as though you were her very own.

"I remember that when I prayed I asked, as did Hezekiah, not for a long life for her, but for fifteen years. I want you to remember this, for all along mamma felt in her heart that this was to be the exact time given to her—just fifteen years, and no more.

"When she became so ill with what the doctors learned too late was pellagra, she talked to me about John's birth fifteen years ago and about the added time the Lord had given to her. Then we both prayed earnestly that she might be spared again to us. Somehow I could never add, 'Nevertheless, not my will, but Thine, O Lord, be done.' Whenever I'd get to that part my tongue would just seem to choke me, and the words wouldn't come out. I wanted so desperately for her to stay with us; I felt I couldn't let her go.

"All this time she kept getting thinner and thinner, and she had such a high fever that her skin was burned brown. Her weight dropped from two hundred pounds to ninety-eight; she was in constant pain.

67

"After the doctors had called in several visiting specialists from the United States they learned that mamma had what is known as pellagra. This, they said, is a disease caused by lack of vitamins, and mamma's was the first case to be known in Canada or the northern United States. But by this time, although they at last knew what to do to help other sufferers, it was too late to do anything for mamma. Still I kept on praying that her life would be spared.

"Then one night I had a dream. Now, all of you children know I don't believe much in ordinary dreams. In fact, I scarcely dream at all. But my dream on that night was as real as anything I've ever known.

"I dreamed that as I knelt at mamma's bedside a voice spoke to me. It said, 'Pray unselfishly. Pray not that your will be done but that His will be done. Only then can the Lord guide and direct you in His path.'

"When I awoke I got up and fell on my knees beside my bed. I said my usual prayer, but this time, instead of demanding that mamma's life be lengthened, I ended my prayer just as I had been told to do in my dream. I said, 'Nevertheless, not my will, but Thine, O Lord, be done.'

"When I rose I quickly dressed and hurried toward the hospital for our usual early-morning visit. But I was still a block away when Annie came flying down the steps, looking for me. 'Hurry, Papa,' she called. 'Mamma's going. Hurry as fast as you can.'

"I ran up the steps and into mamma's room. But when I got there she was gone. In spite of the awful shock I could feel nothing but gladness that her suffering was over. She looked peaceful and calm lying there; her face had an expression that reminded me of mamma in the old days when she was well and strong.

"And then I realized that, just at the very moment I had ended my prayer, mamma had slipped away from us. It had been my dearest wish to keep her here, even though she could never again be well and strong. My selfish prayer had only lengthened her suffering. But when I left the matter in the Lord's hands He saw that it was best to lay her to rest, hard though it is for us to go on without her.

"I've told you this because that is what mamma would have wanted me to do. All her life she was a firm believer in prayer; she always said that every prayer she ever uttered was answered. It was not always answered in the way she might have wished, but it was answered in the way the Lord saw best. I remember that as troublesome matters worked out, mamma would always nod her head and say, 'Well, Papa, as usual the Lord knew best.'

"One of mamma's last wishes was that each of you would go ahead and make something worth while of himself. She mentioned you in particular, John, as the one who should have medical training. But above all, she wanted each of you to live a good, clean life, to trust in the Lord, and to remember that, after all, 'He knows best.'"

John's heart was too full for words. As soon as papa finished he slipped away from the questioning group and hurried outside, behind the big poplar tree in the back yard. As he leaned against its rough bark he thought again of the days when mamma had been home and they had sometimes sat for a few brief moments under this very tree. In memory he could hear her voice as she spoke to him.

"Always be a good boy, John. Do what is right. Help those about you as you strive for an education. And above all, remember your heavenly Father, without whose help you can do nothing."

John lifted his face toward the white clouds overhead. Although he knew that mamma couldn't hear him he felt comforted to speak the words aloud.

"I'll remember, Mamma. I'll do as you told me to do. And thank you, Mamma, for everything."

Chapter 7
The Dollar Dentist

D O YOU think we'll get to Battleford Academy today, Papa?" John eagerly leaned forward from the back seat of the rickety model-T Ford as he tried in vain to look through the swirling dust clouds ahead of them. Dimly he heard his father's voice above the noise of the chugging car.

"*Thump—bump*—think we'll get—*bumpety bump*—there this—*thump*—afternoon," he yelled over his shoulder—"*Bumpety bump*—if this car holds—*thump—thump*—together—*BOOM!*"

"Another tire!" groaned Walter and John.

"Hop out, boys. We'll have to patch it and hope it'll hold for the last few miles. This 250-mile trip from Swift Current has used up all our inner tubes and tire patches except this one. If it blows out, we'll have to walk." Papa spoke mournfully as he climbed stiffly out of the seat and reached for the jack.

John and Walter reluctantly pulled themselves loose from the mountains of luggage piled around them—bundles, bedding, a small trunk, suitcases, and the huge lunch box that Linda had filled to the brim as a safeguard against starvation.

As they worked swiftly they wondered whether it could really be true that they had almost reached

71

their goal. Each one thought of the past months of work in kind Farmer Meileke's harvest fields and of their hard-earned three hundred dollars for school tuition now tucked neatly away in papa's worn billfold.

John scarcely dared breathe as the car rocked and steamed the remainder of the way to Battleford Academy. Before either he or Walter could realize that they were actually there, papa had introduced them to Principal Degering, met the business manager, and paid down their precious money as a deposit on their yearly school bill. Then they realized that papa was actually going; he was leaving them in this strange place without further advice. They exchanged bewildered glances as he kissed each one in turn.

"Good-by, Walter. Good-by, John. Be good boys. Study hard and work hard like your mamma wanted you to do. If you do that, you'll get along all right. I wish I had the money to help you, but all I can give you is my blessing. However, you can work here at school and you can work every summer at Rudolph Meileke's. So you should be able to go through the academy if you really want to do so."

As the supper bell rang John and Walter hurried to their bare dormitory room, shrinking from the curious stares of their jostling schoolmates.

"Do you want to go down to that place they call the cafeteria?" Walter questioned as soon as he had shut their door tightly behind him. "I'm hungry but not hungry enough to go down there and have everybody watch me. Besides, I don't know what you do in a cafeteria. Do you, John?"

"Who, me?" the surprised John answered. "Why, no, of course I don't. From what one of the boys said you walk around here and there to get your food. But he didn't say what you put it on or where to get knives and forks. No, I don't want to go down either. I'd feel awfully strange. We'll finish up the food in our lunch box. We've got enough for a week."

But at the end of three days the boys had choked down the last dried crumb of the once-tasty home-cooked food and had been forced into making their first trip to the dining room.

"After all," Walter said hungrily, as the smell of cooking drifted up from the kitchen below, "we can't stay up here like starved rats in a hole. If we don't eat pretty soon, we'll turn into mummies. I'm so full of dry crumbs right now that I rattle when I walk. Come on. I guess it can't be too bad down there."

After that the boys never missed a meal if they could help it; soon they found themselves well adjusted to the busy, happy life at the academy.

Almost before they realized that the first school year was over, they were once again working in the broad Canadian harvest fields. And once more fall found them back at Battleford, preparing to take up their studies. True, Walter dropped out now and then, for he was not so keenly interested in school-work as was John. But he always came back, so that the brothers spent most of their school years together.

He Never Forgot the Bitterly Cold Days
He Spent Cutting Wood for Hours

Before John could realize the swiftness of time he had finished his junior year with the office of class president, spent another summer at Meileke's, and had returned for fall registration. His heart beat high as he entered the business office to sign as a senior student. But he was due for a rude shock. Startled, he looked up to see the business manager slowly shaking his head.

"I'm sorry, John, but I don't see how we can possibly let you register. Though you've paid up your last year's school bill with this summer's wages, you have only twenty dollars left toward your senior year expenses. I'm afraid you'd never be able to pay off such a big debt. Since our school operates on a very small amount of money we must have cash payments. That's why I'll have to say no."

John stared blankly at the manager. For a moment it seemed that surely he was talking to someone else—not to John Orlando Neufeld, who had come back to Battleford Academy to graduate with his class.

"But—but—I have to graduate. I've worked all these years so I could finish school. You—you've *got* to let me, Mr. Edstrom. Please let me. I'll do anything you say. Why, I promised my mother I'd go on to school and graduate. You—you've just got to let me."

John never knew whether it was his earnest, shaking voice or his tear-filled eyes that won Mr. Edstrom's grudging consent for him to enroll in school. But one thing he did know: During the school year he cut two hundred cords of wood with

75

his nicked old ax, hauled coal, and did small extra jobs around the school. He did all this in addition to his studies. He never forgot the bitterly cold days when, after cutting wood for hours, he would come in and try to practice his typing with his fingers as stiff and lifeless as though they were lumps of ice.

As spring drew near his high hopes increased. The business manager had called him into the office and told him he was going to be allowed to graduate in June. His teachers had told him his grades were satisfactory. John felt that at last his goal was in sight.

Then he learned his tonsils would have to be removed. After years of colds and sore throats he found that his infected tonsils must be taken out at once.

Someone told him of the only "doctor" near enough for him to visit, but warned, "He charges thirty-five dollars, and he won't do a thing for you unless you pay cash." John could never quite remember how he got the money. But, here a little, there a little, he earned and borrowed that precious thirty-five dollars and took it with him for his operation.

"I'll wait out here for you," Principal Degering said as John got out of the car in front of the doctor's house. "You won't need me in there. The doctor will give you some sort of local anesthetic. You won't feel any pain at all. Then when you're ready I'll take you home and see that you get to bed for a day or so."

John hoped that Mr. Degering was right. But as he looked at the towering giant in front of him and heard his rough voice demand his fee in advance, his courage began to fade away.

"Sit down on that kitchen stool," barked the doctor. "Now open your mouth. Hm! Novocain wouldn't do no good in them rotten tonsils. No use to waste it on 'em.

"They should've been out a long time ago. Here, boy. Open your mouth. Wider. Now hang onto that stool for all you're worth. I'm going to start cuttin'. I'll have 'em out in a jiffy."

Tears streamed down John's agonized face as the doctor carved four great pieces of tonsil from his bleeding throat. Each time the knife approached, his fingers dug deeper into the stool until he felt that surely he had left his fingerprints deep in the hard wood.

As he stumbled away from the house he was thankful for Mr. Degering's strong arm and kind help to aid him in getting back to his room and into bed. For days he lay there, too ill to eat, his throat a burning misery that tormented him day and night. In fact, he had been up only a short while before his father stopped for a brief visit.

"My boy!" he heard papa exclaim. "What in the world has happened to you! You're as thin as a rail."

As John mumbled the account of the so-called operation he saw his father's face turn red with anger, though he said never a word. But John felt oddly comforted as papa slipped his arm around John's thin shoulders and gave him a little hug.

"You must rest until you're stronger, John," he warned, "even though you'll have a great deal of schoolwork to make up. You must rest until you're well. I'm sorry you've had such an experience. I only wish I could help pay your way, but I just don't have the money. A minister's salary is small, as you well know. And mine has always had to stretch a long, long way.

"I'm proud of you for the way you've gone ahead and earned your expenses through school. Now you've caught up with Wilfred; you two will graduate together in June. Though Walter's missed some schoolwork, he'll be able to graduate later on too.

"Mary, Katie, Caroline, Jake, Nettie, Bertha, Dave, Annie, and Linda are all happily married. Annie's a fine trained nurse. Sarah, Mildred, and Rolland are doing well at the school in Swift Current.

"Yes," added papa. "You've all done real well. Mamma'd be proud of you if she could only be here to see you children." John saw unaccustomed tears in his father's eyes, and as they kissed in farewell, neither could say a word.

But that evening, when John opened his Bible to study his Old Testament history lesson, he found a crisp new dollar bill tucked away at the very last chapter of Lamentations. He thought that surely this was a fitting place for the money.

John thought too that never had any dollar bill looked brighter or more inviting than this one gift that his father had been able to give him. A thousand places for its use flashed through his mind: a new shirt for graduation, or a pair of half soles for his worn shoes, or new socks and ties to brighten his shabby wardrobe. Gently he fingered papa's loving gift.

But then he shook his head as he carefully replaced the dollar bill. Only this time he put it toward the first pages of Genesis.

"That's the place for it," he thought. "I'm all through with sorrowful Lamentations, and soon I'll be starting out on Genesis. That means "a beginning."

"I'm going to do what mamma always wanted me to do. After I graduate from here I'm going on to college. Then I'm going to dental school. I don't know how I'll pay my way, but I'll manage somehow. Then perhaps I can do something to help people who are sick and suffering, and really heal them—not "butcher" them as that doctor "butchered" me.

"I'll keep papa's dollar until I'm ready to begin dental school," he added, as he gently closed his worn Bible. "Then I'll use it as part of my tuition. I'll work hard so that I can make papa proud of me."

His brown eyes looked far, far away into the distant past. His lips moved noiselessly. Softly he murmured, "And someday I know I'll meet mamma once again. She'll put her arms around me to tell me how glad she is to see me. I want to live and to work so that when she does I can hear her voice say, 'John, my boy, I'm proud of my dollar dentist.'"

Karen Sat Motionless, Praying That Ronnie Would Not Waken

Chapter 8
Karen and the Cobra

"OH, PLEASE let me bathe the baby. I'll take good care of him. Truly I will, Aunt Marie. I know exactly what to do. Please let me bathe him and put him to bed today." Karen's brown eyes pleaded until their soft shining earnestness won Mrs. Drayson's reluctant consent.

"All right, dear," she said smilingly. "Perhaps this is a good time to let you take care of Ronnie. I'm going to be very busy for the next two or three hours. This afternoon our newly organized Mothers' Society will meet for the first time, and there are several last-minute tasks that must be done. I'll have to take the servants with me to help put the meeting room in order.

"Before I leave I'll mix the formula for baby's milk so that it will be all bottled and ready for his feeding right after bath time. I do hope he'll go right to sleep as soon as he's put in his crib. For the past two or three weeks he's been so restless after his feedings that I've been worried. I hate to see him toss and tumble; he used to sleep so well I can't imagine what's wrong."

Karen's face was troubled as kind Mrs. Drayson left the room to get baby Ronnie. She wanted to do all that she could to be of help to this busy woman who was really no relative at all, but who had welcomed Karen when the young girl's missionary parents had been killed by bandits. She longed to repay both Mr. and Mrs. Drayson for their loving-kindness in caring for her until distant relatives in the States could be found. She knew how patient and understanding they had been with her all during these months when she had seemed dazed by the awful tragedy.

Karen's thin brown hands trembled with eagerness as she lifted laughing, roly-poly Ronnie from his buggy and carried him carefully to the towel-covered table. Her throat felt tight and choked as she undressed the gurgling baby and slowly lowered him into his small tin bathtub. She knew how very dear he was to Aunt Marie and Uncle John. From the servants she had learned of the two little graves far away in another lonely corner of China—two little graves where Ronnie's older brothers lay sleeping. And she knew that Ronnie, who had been born during the past year, seemed almost a miracle to his parents.

"There, darling. Now you're all ready to be fed. But I'm not going to let you stuff yourself this time. No, I'm not. Daddy always said that too much food gave little babies bad tummy-aches. Now let Karen hold you. Oh, but you're a precious baby. How I wish you were my very own brother!"

Karen's thin arms tightened longingly around the soap-and-talcum-scented bundle as her brown eyes looked straight down into the round blue eyes staring so trustingly up into hers.

Squeak! Creak! Squeak! Creak! The little hand-made rocker sang its own lullaby as the two rocked back and forth, back and forth. The battered kitchen clock ticked on and on until Karen saw that at last Ronnie's long black lashes lay fringed against his pink cheeks.

"He's asleep. He's really gone to sleep," Karen thought triumphantly. "Now if I can just tuck him into his crib without waking him, how happy Aunt Marie will be!"

Carefully she pulled herself out of the little chair and tiptoed to the door. Holding Ronnie against her shoulder, she walked quietly down the long hallway and into the clean plain nursery. Karen scarcely dared breathe as she gently, ever so gently, lowered the sleeping baby into his small crib. But at last she felt his little body firm against the cool sheets and carefully pulled her hand from under his back. Then, as she bent to cover him she saw his eyelids flutter open, his blue eyes look into hers, and his little mouth draw down into a sad pucker.

"Oh, Ronnie," she wailed. "I thought you were sound asleep. There, there, honey, never mind. Karen'll sit right over here in this chair by the window. Now be a good boy and close your eyes."

Tucking the covers around the chubby, restless little body, Karen tiptoed to the big bamboo chair by the window and sat down. The room was cool and still, and the longer Karen sat there, the sleepier she became. From time to time she glanced at Ronnie, only to find him still wide-eyed, moving his head from side to side or staring in wonder at his newly discovered fists.

At last, as she saw his eyelids growing heavier and heavier, she slumped against the chair back and thought drowsily that surely he would be asleep in just a moment. Karen never knew just why she awoke at that exact instant. It could not have been a noise, for the horrible thing in the doorway moved too stealthily to have aroused her. It could not have been any spoken warning, for the silence of the house lay thick upon her as she realized that she and the helpless baby were the only ones in the dwelling. It could not have been the distant rise and fall of the servants' voices as they hurried back and forth in the mission compound, for she had heard them long before she fell asleep.

As Karen looked at wide-eyed Ronnie, she shivered as though struck by an icy wind, even though perspiration beaded her forehead.

"O dear God," she prayed, "let Ronnie go to sleep. Please, please, dear God, make him go to sleep right now."

Karen's fingernails bit into her palms as she tensely watched the hideous yellow-brown thing slide sinuously over the floor. She saw it speed straight as an arrow toward Ronnie's crib, stopping only once to rear high above the floor, its round, bronze-colored eyes staring directly at her. She felt like screaming as, bit by bit, it coiled itself around one leg of the crib and then flowed upward and onto the white spread.

"A cobra! It can't be—but it is! It's a cobra!" Karen thought wildly. Vivid mental pictures of cobra-bitten men and women flashed dizzily through her mind and shattered into one dreadful scene of Ronnie dying in agony from the snake's venomous bite. She knew that any movement would bring an instant attack from the reptile, for when a cobra is aroused it becomes very vicious. And she knew that, to an unreasoning snake, the waving of those dimpled baby arms would be the signal for an instant attack.

"Oh, if I could only *do* something!" Karen thought desperately, well aware that she dared not move a muscle lest she bring death to both Ronnie and herself. "If I could only do something to save Ronnie. Dear God. Help me! Show me what to do."

"Pray, my child; pray!" Karen's eyes opened wide, for she knew that no human being except Ronnie was in the room with her. She quivered as the voice continued softly:

"Thou shalt tread upon the lion and adder.... Because he hath set his love upon me, therefore will I deliver him.... He shall call upon me, and I will answer him: I will be with him in trouble; I will deliver him, and honour him.

"And all things, whatsoever ye shall ask in prayer, believing, ye shall receive."

Karen closed her eyes and prayed earnestly-prayed as she had never prayed before, even when kneeling beside some of daddy's desperately ill patients. And when she again opened her eyes to look at Ronnie, she saw him lying quietly, ever so quietly asleep, while curled round and round upon his body lay the hideous coiled death.

The clock ticked on and on. Karen dared not turn her head but out of the corner of her eye she saw the clock hands move slowly around. One hour! Karen felt that surely she had been there for days instead of just one hour. And then she heard stealthy tiptoed footsteps down the hall. She dared not move. She dared not call out a warning. She prayed.

"Has he gone to sleep? I'm sorry I was gone so long," Aunt Marie whispered quietly from the doorway. "Did you—oh!" her soft voice stopped abruptly, cut off in the middle of a sentence. Karen sat motionless, praying, praying, praying that Ronnie would not awaken, would not move, would not cry out in his sleep. Dimly she was aware of Ronnie's mother, leaning rigidly against the doorway, her face as white as the bleached muslin sheet that covered the sleeping baby.

Pictures whirled dizzily through Karen's mind. She thought wildly that this was like a game of statue that she had once played with visiting children from the United States. She remembered how they had formed a line, hand in hand, with the strongest child in the lead. He had swung them about until, one by one, they had tumbled loose and "frozen" into that exact position for a moment or so. But Karen knew only too well that this was not a game. It was life and death, with helpless little Ronnie as the principal character.

Karen heard the clock tick on and on, on and on. She saw Ronnie's mother move backward, inch by inch. She moved so slowly that she seemed not to be moving at all, until she finally disappeared from sight down the hall without even a whisper of sound to betray her going.

Tick! Tock! Tick! Tock! On and on dragged the hands of the clock. Still and quiet lay Ronnie's dimpled hands.

Still and deadly quiet lay the creeping death upon Ronnie's precious little body. Another fifteen minutes, thirty minutes, another hour.

"O God," Karen breathed silently, "hear my prayers. Spare Ronnie. Save us, save us, please, dear God."

As tears blurred her eyes she saw the snake stir, move sluggishly, and slither toward the edge of the crib. Karen scarcely breathed as it slid down to the floor and glided straight toward the hallway. She dared not move even as it neared the door and the watchful Draysons.

"There! Careful. Look out!" rang the cries of the faithful servants summoned by Aunt Marie.

"Hit it! Quick!" Karen heard Mr. Drayson's voice above the dull thud of the hastily-grabbed garden tools as willing hands lifted them and struck again and again at the writhing yellowish-brown coils of death.

She tried to rise from her cramped position, but her legs and arms felt limp and useless. Dazedly she watched Mrs. Drayson rush frantically to the crib and snatch up sleeping Ronnie.

"My baby! My precious baby! You're safe. Oh, thank God, you're safe," she cried. Karen saw the joyful tears streaming down Aunt Marie's face. She felt Uncle John's strong arms lifting her gently from her chair and heard his kind voice urging her to try to walk. Distantly she heard him speak, but his words sounded faint and far away.

"You've been a brave girl. We owe Ronnie's life to you."

Then Karen heard nothing but a great rushing sound and saw nothing but a swirling blackness that wrapped itself tightly around her and pulled her down, down into complete darkness.

The light pressed against Karen's eyelids as a gurgling laugh sounded close beside her ear.

"Karen. Karen, dear. Wake up." Karen's eyes opened in dizzy surprise.

"Why—where—where am I?" she gasped, staring at Mr. and Mrs. Drayson and baby Ronnie. "What happened—oh! I know." Then as remembrance flooded back she shuddered. "Oh! It was awful. I lived a lifetime in those two hours!" She smiled wanly up at her friends, speaking words that she had not been able to say for weeks past.

"Daddy always used to call me his praying missionary, because I'd pray by the bedside for the sick babies. Our favorite texts were the ones I said over and over today. Daddy told me those promises had saved many, many sick children when he could do nothing more for them. And today they saved Ronnie."

Mrs. Drayson wiped away her fast falling tears as she bent to kiss Karen. "We can never thank you enough for your Christian faith and courage, my dear, and for your love for Ronnie. But now you must rest, for you have had a dreadful experience.

"However, we can't wait to tell you that we want you to stay with us until time for you to go away to school. Ronnie needs a sister like you, and we need a daughter. Will you belong to us, my dear?"

Karen felt her throat too full for words. But her glad cry as she reached for baby Ronnie and held him tight against her was her joyous unspoken answer.

"I'm Going to Turn Around and Let My
Legs Dangle Outside," Said June

Chapter 9
Scarred for Life

"O GWENDOLEN, we're going to have fun today. I only wish you could go on our seventh-grade picnic with us," June said excitedly.

She hastily wrapped the last nut-bread sandwich and squeezed it into the tin lunch pail on the very top of all the other delicious home-cooked food. She thought how good it would taste at noon; fat whole-wheat bread-and-jelly sandwiches, round orange-nut-bread sandwiches, plump black olives and tiny sweet pickles from papa's general merchandise store, and generous slices of sister Helen's rich chocolate cake.

"I wish I could too, but I can't. I'm only in the sixth grade. But I'll be here by the time you're home, so that you can tell me all about your trip," Gwendolen answered. "Do you think you'll get back by five o'clock, Juney?"

"I'm sure we will. Our teacher told us we'd try to return about four-thirty. She said she didn't want to be out too late with a big hayrack full of youngsters."

"No, and I don't blame her one bit either. I wouldn't want the responsibility of taking them in the first place," soberly added Mother Dalton. The surprised girls saw that her usually smiling face looked grave.

"Don't act so worried, Mamma," June spoke hastily. "Why, we've got a good driver, and his horses are as gentle as can be.

"Besides, we're only going three or four miles from town. We'll spend the day in Willow Grove and build a big bonfire on the riverbank so that we can toast marshmallows."

"Well, just the same, I can't help worrying," Mother Dalton continued. "I think this is the first class picnic to be held so far from Burns and the first wagon ride for such a large group. You'll be squeezed together like sardines."

"Well, if we are, some of us can be good little sardines. We'll sit along the sides of the wagon so that our legs can hang over the edge. That'll be more fun than crowding together in the middle anyway," June laughed.

"Now, June, listen to me," Mother Dalton warned. "You must promise me that whatever you do, you will not sit near the edge of the wagon. That is very dangerous. The horses might become frightened and run away. Or you might be caught on the side of the wagon and dragged along. I have known of several very serious accidents that happened in just such a manner."

"I'll be careful, Mamma. Really I will. After all, I'm not a baby any more. I can take care of myself!" June answered almost sharply, impatient to be on her way to the appointed meeting place.

Giving her mother a hasty kiss, June grabbed

her broad-brimmed straw hat and tin lunch bucket, and hurried out the door after Gwendolen. It was not until the white picket gate had swung shut behind them that June spoke.

"Whew! I was afraid that mamma'd call me back and make me promise point blank not to sit on the side of the wagon. And that's exactly what some of us want to do. Frank said it's lots of fun. He said he'd ridden that way ever so many times on his uncle's hayrack."

"But isn't it really dangerous?" Gwendolen questioned anxiously. "It would be dreadful if anything went wrong and you got hurt. O Juney! I couldn't stand that." Tears sprang to her blue eyes as she looked at her friend.

June laughed gaily as she flung her arms around her chum and gave her a hug.

"Now, don't be a fraidy cat! Nothing's going to happen except things that are fun. And I'll be back this afternoon to tell you all about our seventh-grade picnic."

Gwendolen tried to look cheerful as she waved good-by, but her lips stopped smiling as soon as June rounded the corner on Main Street. She tried hard to feel that all would be well with the day's outing, but deep down inside she wished wholeheartedly that June had listened more closely to Mother Dalton.

But June was not at all worried. She hurried breathlessly on her way, quite unmindful of her mother's warning, intent only on the fun-filled hours ahead.

"Well, you're here at last. Now we can start," called Hazel. "We were beginning to wonder what had happened to you."

"Nothing happened," June sang out. "I just stopped to talk with Gwendolen for a few minutes. I'm all ready. Where's the wagon?"

"Listen and you'll hear the team coming now," Frank answered.

Amid choking dust swirls the big team of horses pulled the heavy wagon into view. With wild cries of joy the entire seventh-grade class clambered aboard and chose places for the gala ride.

"Please, boys and girls, when you sit down be careful to stay away from the edge of the wagon," the teacher warned. "Although the horses are very gentle, it is still possible that they could become frightened. Since I'm responsible for your safety today I want to be very sure that you run no risks."

All during the ride several of the boys grumbled that "there's always something to take the joy out of life." But June saw that they, as well as the rest of the class, carefully followed their teacher's advice and crowded together toward the center of the wagon bed.

June thought she had never had so much fun. The ride itself was thrilling, with the horse-drawn wagon lumbering along over the rutted road, past the tree-shaded Silvies River, up the steep gray sagebrush hills, and down into the green meadows of Willow Grove.

The picnickers agreed that their camp treat of marshmallows toasted golden brown over the campfire's red coals was surely a perfect dessert for a delicious noon meal. One and all moaned that they were simply too stuffed to play any more games. But soon they began to run wildly here and there in the willow clumps, playing blindman's buff, black man, and run, sheep, run.

"Oh! I hate to leave," sighed June as she and Frances and Hazel gathered up their lunch pails and climbed wearily into the waiting wagon. "Hasn't it been fun?"

"It certainly has," Hazel groaned, "but I'm so stiff and sore from running that I can hardly move. My! but we'll all be tired tomorrow!"

"Well, we don't have to go to school until afternoon to get our report cards," Frances said cheerily. "So we can all sleep late in the morning."

"Yes, and I'm certainly going to," agreed June. "Gwendolen's going to stay all night at my house, and we'll probably talk so long about the picnic that we won't wake up very early in the morning.

"But say, girls, I expect I will get up fairly early, after all. I almost forgot that papa told me to come over to the store by nine o'clock. He wants me to look at some catalog pictures of high-laced hiking boots. He's half-promised me a pair for my thirteenth birthday, June 1. And how I hope I get them to wear on our Campfire girls camping trip!"

"All aboard, everybody. We're late now," called out their smiling classmate, Harley, who had won permission to drive part of the way home. "Hurry up. Here we go."

Quickly the girls took the same places they had occupied on the morning ride. With increasing weariness they watched as the lengthening shadows forecast the fast-falling eastern Oregon dusk.

"I'm so tired I can't stand up a minute longer. I'm going to sit down," June said.

"Where?" inquired Hazel. "All the places in the middle of the wagon are taken."

"Then I'll sit down right here," June replied. "Why can't we sit cross-legged and lean back against each other? That wouldn't be quite so tiresome as standing up for another two miles."

"Well, we can try, but it doesn't look as though there'd be much room," Hazel answered doubtfully.

June soon learned that Hazel was right. For squirm and turn as they could, they found no place for their knees without poking them into their classmates' backs.

"I'm going to turn around and let my legs dangle outside," June finally announced in disgust. "I'll have to stand up if I don't, and I'm simply too tired to do that."

"All right! Then I will too," Hazel agreed, and soon whispers of "Me too" were heard, as weary picnickers stretched their cramped legs over the wagon's edge and let them dangle limply.

"Better be careful, or teacher'll see us!" warned Frank in a low voice. "You know she said not to do this, and the driver'd make us stop in a minute."

"Oh, teacher's too tired even to turn around to look at us. And the driver's so busy watching Harley that he's not paying any attention either," June scoffed. "Anyway, what in the world could possibly happen to us out here on this country road? There isn't a thing that could hurt us. It'll be all—"

June felt the words jerked right out of her mouth as the frightened horses shied at a coiled rattlesnake, and the heavy wagon lurched toward the side of the lane.

"Hang on! Hang on tight," she heard the driver yell frantically. As he grabbed the reins she saw that he and Harley were both pulling with all their might against the plunging, rearing horses.

"Whoa there! Whoa!" she heard him shout above the children's frightened screams as they hastily scrambled away from the wagon's edge and toward the center safety zone.

As June tried desperately to loosen herself from her wedged-in position she felt the wagon slide sickeningly off the dirt road. Her terrified eyes stared in unbelieving horror as it swung in a deadly arc. Closer, ever closer it came to the cruel barbed-wire fence that at this exact spot ran close beside the country lane.

Frantically she pushed against the wooden sideboards. But even as her muscles strained with the effort, she knew despairingly that it was no use—no use at all. She saw that she was trapped— trapped as in a vise—with the tearing wire barbs coming nearer and nearer.

And then June felt a dreadful tearing, searing agony across her legs. "Help!" she screamed. "Help! I'm caught in the barbed wire." But her voice was lost in the shouts and yells of the frightened seventh-grade pupils, whose eyes were turned toward the straining horses.

One! Two! Three! June felt herself dragged along the wire and against three fence posts. Then great waves of pain swept over her and drowned the liquid fire in her bleeding legs.

June never knew when the white-faced drivers pulled the lathered horses to a full stop. From a great distance she heard the hushed voices of her classmates and teacher as they gently lifted her up onto the wagon and bent over the terrible gaping wounds almost encircling her legs. Fragments of their tearful conversation swirled dizzily through her head. She thought how strange it was to hear them speak so pityingly of someone named June Dalton.

"We must get her to a doctor at once!"

"Poor child! I'm afraid she'll never walk again."

"She'll be in bed for months and months. Oh, it's dreadful!"

"Shouldn't we do something to stop the bleeding? Look! The barbed wire caught her right below the knees."

Just as the wagon started on its swift jolting ride to Burns, June gritted her teeth and rolled over onto her stomach. Dimly she realized that if she must spend months in bed she could not permit her back to be bruised from the wagon's jolting. She could never quite remember that terrible ride or how long it took to reach her white-faced mother and the sober-faced doctors who stood beside her hastily moved bed in the big front parlor.

She knew only that before she floated into complete unconsciousness she must speak to them. She must tell Mother Dalton how sorry she was to have ruined the crisp new gingham school dress and the long black cotton stockings, now torn to shreds. Vaguely she remembered hearing that one should never eat a meal before taking an anesthetic. Her thick tongue struggled to warn them.

"I—I ate——" she gasped.

"Now, now, June. Just lie still," warned kind Dr. Griffith while Dr. Saurman carefully adjusted the chloroform mask. "Don't try to talk."

"Marshmallows! I ate 'em!" June's voice croaked triumphantly, and then she felt herself shooting out into a whirling boundless space full of shining stars.

June never knew when a sobbing Gwendolen was turned away from her door that evening. Nor did she hear the tearful voices of Father and Mother Dalton after their talk with the doctors.

"I can't bear it, Mamma," wept Mr. Dalton. "Just think! Our girl was going to have her hiking boots for a birthday present. She wanted those more than anything in the world. But what good will boots do her if the doctors have to amputate one leg!"

"They can't, Jim. We can't let them do it today. I know they're good doctors and they've done all they can, but still she's burning up with fever. I'm going to ask them to wait until tomorrow to decide.

"Tomorrow all the school children of every church are meeting together for prayer for June's recovery. They themselves have asked the ministers to arrange for this special service. Surely their faith will be rewarded. We *must* wait!"

Long weeks afterward, when June was safely out of the "Valley of the Shadow" she heard the story of the churches' special services, when the prayers of all the school children and their parents ascended in her behalf. June felt the tears streaking down her pale cheeks as she listened. But they were happy tears, for by now she knew that she would walk again and that she would be able to wear the beautiful new boots that papa had placed so proudly on the table near her bed.

June felt that she could never repay everyone for all that they had done. She thought of the faithful doctors, her kind mother and father, her older sisters and brothers, the school friends who so faithfully visited her, and little sister Mildred, who cheerfully gave up her tomboyish out-of-doors fun to stay indoors all that beautiful summer and play games and "paper dolls" with the invalid.

She knew that she would never forget any of these friends. But she was especially grateful to the Byrd sisters—Evelyn, Marjorie, and Gladys—who played the violin and piano, and sang like real songbirds; to Laura Thornburg, who made countless trips to the library for good books, and to thoughtful Mrs. Lampshire, who almost daily brought delicious tray surprises of specially prepared food from her home next door.

But when her entire seventh-grade class came for a very quiet belated surprise birthday party, June felt that she could wish for nothing more.

"It's wonderful to have such good friends and to know that soon I'll be able to be up on crutches," she said that evening to Gwendolen, who had run over for her usual after-supper visit. "I can hardly realize even yet that I'm really going to be all right."

She flinched as Gwendolen leaned over and gently touched the deep red scars that almost encircled June's legs.

"Will they always show, June?" she asked sorrowfully. "Yes, those scars will always show. And for a long time they'll be more or less painful, the doctors said. But I'm so thankful to have my legs that I wouldn't dare complain. It makes me shudder to think how near I came to losing them.

"You know, Gwendolen, you were right that day of the picnic when you felt that something was going to happen to me. Oh, I don't mean that you could look into the future, but you knew how rude I was to mamma when she warned me to be careful. You didn't have to think very hard to know that an accident might happen."

"I guess things always go wrong when we disobey our parents," Gwendolen soberly remarked.

"Well, I've learned my lesson the hard way," June added. "Believe me, from now on whenever I think of going against mother's wishes I'll just look down at these awful scars. They'll be warning enough for me. I'll never disobey again."

In a Few Minutes She Found Herself in Front of a Brown House

Chapter 10
The Ghost in the Parlor

I DON'T care. I want to go!" stormed Marilyn. "All the other girls in my room have been invited too, and *their* mothers'll let them go to the slumber party." Tears of self-pity filled her resentful brown eyes and splashed unheeded on her new silk blouse.

"Did your invitation say it was only a slumber party?" mother asked gently. A hurt little frown creased her forehead as she watched her daughter's unusual display of temper.

"O Mother, you know what the invitation said as well as I do," Marilyn exclaimed pettishly. "First we're to have dinner at Jane's house. Then her mother's going to take all of us to a real fortune teller to have our fortunes told. It'll be perfectly thrilling. She's actually a clair—clair—"

"Clairvoyant?" smiled patient mother.

"I guess that's what she's called. Anyway, Jane's mother says she's a real medium, and she can tell wonderful fortunes. I just can't miss such an exciting Halloween party. Please, Mother. Please let me go," Marilyn begged.

"Why can't Marilyn go to the party?" questioned little Stephen. "Has she been naughty?"

"No, dear, she's been a good girl. But neither daddy nor I approve of school-night slumber parties for these young girls who are just Marilyn's age. If the invitation were for an early dinner hour and a few games afterward I'd be glad to let her go. But it would be unthinkable to permit her to visit a medium, and that trip is to be the evening's entertainment."

"Why not?" sniffed Marilyn, her tearful attention caught by the solemn note in mother's voice. "I can't see any harm in going there for fun. It's just a joke. After all, no one's really going to believe anything she tells us."

Marilyn and Stephen watched as mother sank into a nearby rocker and slowly shook her head.

"No, dear, you must write a nice little note to thank Jane for the invitation. But you must tell her that you cannot come. However, I think that you should know why I feel so strongly on this subject.

"Sit down, both of you. Then I'll tell you this story as it was told to me many years ago by a very talented young woman who was at that time a member of my college music group. She was a real Christian—a young person who was not given to foolish fears. That is why this story of her night of terror has always remained so plainly in my mind.

"Elsie was extremely fond of good music and loved to hear the great artists. However, she was working her way through college. She had no money with which to buy tickets for the many fine programs given in the large city nearby," mother began.

104

"Neither had the young college men of her acquaintance extra money for such entertainments. Consequently, for months Elsie had to try to content herself with reading newspaper notices about the artists who played and sang in the concert series.

"Therefore it wasn't at all strange that, when she was introduced to a nice-appearing young man employed near the school, she began after a time to accept his invitations. She was never disappointed when she spent an evening with him, for not only was he polite and thoughtful but he always took her to a really worth-while concert or lecture.

"As the months sped rapidly by they became quite good friends. But Elsie could not help noticing that in spite of their friendship he had never invited her to his home. She knew he had a mother, although he rarely spoke of her. In fact, he seemed not to hear Elsie's quite broad hints that she would like to meet this other member of his family.

"But at last something happened that made it possible for Elsie actually to meet Bill's mother. And, when she did, she would have given almost anything in the world to have been thousands of miles away. But by that time it was too late."

"Mother!" gasped Marilyn. "What happened?" She leaned tensely forward, Halloween invitation completely forgotten.

"Don't hurry me," smiled mother, looking at Marilyn's worried face and Stephen's round eyes. "I'll tell you the entire story, but you mustn't interrupt. Just listen until I finish.

"At length Bill invited Elsie to go to a very special concert with him. On this date one of the world's most famous symphony orchestras was going to play. The tickets were very expensive, but he made arrangements for them weeks ahead of time. Elsie thought that she could never wait until the day arrived, but at last it did. And then at noon the blow fell. During the lunch hour Bill telephoned and told Elsie that it was necessary for him to work overtime that night.

"'I'm sorry that I can't get away, Elsie,' he said. 'However, I've made arrangements for you to pick up your ticket at the ticket office. They'll keep it for you until eight-thirty. I'm sure you can get down there by that time if you leave the school by six o'clock.'

"'O Bill, what a shame!' Elsie replied. 'It's very kind of you to go to so much trouble, but I couldn't think of going alone. I don't mind the long streetcar trip early in the evening, but I wouldn't want to come home by myself late at night. I wouldn't get back to my landlady's until about one o'clock in the morning, and that's too late on a winter night. I guess I'll just have to miss the program, after all. But thank you anyway.'

"'Wait a minute. Don't hang up,' Bill urged. 'You haven't given me time to finish. Of course, I know it's very informal; you should have a written invitation from mother. But, lacking time to do all that, she told me to invite you to come to our house to spend the night after the concert. Since we live only twelve blocks from the auditorium, you can get there in a couple of minutes by taxi. Mother said it would be very foolish for you to make a long trip across the city on a cold snowy night when you could stay with her.'

"Almost before she knew what she was doing, Elsie had accepted the informal invitation. The hours whirled by until at last the wonderful, wonderful concert was over. Then she was one of the hurrying crowd carried out of the emptying concert hall. Quickly she called a taxicab, and in a few minutes found herself in front of a brown house on a quiet, tree-lined street.

"Elsie's heart beat more quickly as she ran up the icy steps and rang the doorbell. She jumped as the door swung noiselessly open and a soft voice greeted her.

"'Good evening, my dear. Of course you're Elsie. Do come right on in. We've been expecting you!' A small, white-haired lady motioned her into the lonely dimly lighted hall.

"'G—good evening. Is Bill here already? Did you say, "We've been expecting you?"' Elsie stammered, suddenly and strangely ill-at-ease.

"'Oh dear me! Did I? No, Bill won't be home until after twelve. His employer was taken to the hospital today, so that Bill has had to take full charge of the overtime work tonight. He'll be tired when he gets home. But come into the parlor, my dear child. I don't know what I'm thinking of to keep you standing here!

"'Take off your wraps,' Mrs. Gray said. 'I know you must be tired and anxious to get to bed. I'm only sorry that I can't offer you a guest room, but our bed-davenport will have to do. However, it's really very soft and comfortable, and I've spread an extra wool blanket over the foot, in case you're chilly.'

"'Thank you so much, Mrs. Gray,' Elsie said. 'I know that I'll sleep well. And I'm very grateful for your invitation to stay here. Without it I couldn't have gone to the program.'

"'I'm also very glad that you could come,' said her hostess. 'As I mentioned before, one would think that such a large house would have a guest room. But I've had to remodel several of the former upstairs bedrooms into an apartment for my business.

"'Now let me show you the way to the washroom. I've hung your towels on the rack by the mirror. I'll give you my flashlight too, so that you can slip it under your pillow. I know how confusing it is to get up at night in a strange place and try to find the light switch.'

"'Oh, I'm sure I'll rest well,' Elsie answered, eyeing the neatly made bed all ready and waiting for its overnight guest. 'Of course, I probably won't go to sleep right away; I'll be thinking of tonight's program and hearing it all again.'

"'Wouldn't you like a cup of hot milk?' Mrs. Gray asked. 'I'd be glad to bring it to you. Bill usually likes a bite when he comes home late, so I'm used to preparing midnight snacks. However, we won't wait for him. He won't be home for another hour. It's just eleven o'clock now, and I don't expect him until twelve.

"'By the way, Elsie, he'll have to go through this room to get to the kitchen, for our other hallway is being painted. But he'll tiptoe through very quietly so that he won't rouse you. He won't need a light; he could find his way blindfolded, I'm sure. Now shall I bring a hot drink?'

"'Please do, Mrs. Gray,' Elsie answered. 'It's very kind of you. I'm sure that some hot milk would taste good.'

"'Fine! Now get ready for bed. Then when I return you can slip under your quilts and get warm. You'll be able to go to sleep very quickly, I'm sure.'

"Soon Elsie was alone in the big old-fashioned parlor. She leaned back against the plump bed pillows as she gratefully sipped a delicious hot drink from a thin Blue Willow cup. Then she read her evening chapter from her little purse-size Bible and for some unknown reason put the Holy Book at the edge of her pillow instead of back in its leather case.

"'Now I'm going to try to go right to sleep,' Elsie thought as she slipped across the room and clicked off the light switch. 'But somehow I'm not one bit sleepy. I guess the concert was too exciting. Anyhow, I'll be as snug as can be in my soft bed and think back over the program. Ouch!'

"She stumbled as a round object loomed out of the darkness and she bumped full force against its hard surface.

"'Oh dear,' she wailed. 'I should have used that flashlight. I'm all turned around; I forgot all about that little table Mrs. Gray moved away from the bed.

"'And Bill won't know about it either. He'll probably stumble against it and bump his shins too. If I'm still awake when he gets home, I'll call out and warn him to be careful. But I hope I'm asleep by that time.'

"However, try as she would, Elsie could not get to sleep. The bed was soft, the sheets and pillow cases were snowy white and faintly perfumed with lavender, and the woolen coverings were light and warm. But Elsie felt as though something—some unknown danger—was lurking near, drawing ever closer and closer.

"Just as the clock chimed twelve Elsie was glad to hear the front door open. She was glad to feel the blast of crisp cold night air that blew in and followed the echoing footsteps along the hallway and into the musty parlor. She heard them pause for a moment. Then on they came, steadily, heavily, toward the center of the room.

"'Wait, Bill,' Elsie called softly, fearful of waking her hostess in the room above. 'Your mother has pulled the davenport out from the wall and put the little table in the middle of the room. Watch out for it. I bruised my knee when I bumped into it awhile ago.'

"The heavy footsteps came on and on. At last they stopped. Elsie's heart throbbed heavily at the sound of silence.

"'Bill, where are you?' she demanded, half afraid and half angry. 'Don't try to scare me. I know you're there. Your mother told me you'd be home at midnight. Now go on into the kitchen and get your midnight lunch. You won't keep me awake, for I haven't been able to go to sleep.'

"Elsie heard no voice in reply, but again she heard the heavy tread on the carpet. The footsteps moved on, around the table, directly to the edge of her bed.

"'Bill!' Elsie half-screamed. 'What are you doing? Say something to me!'

"But no human sound broke the night stillness in answer to her terrified cry. Elsie heard only the eerie sighing of the winter wind as it moaned around the corners of the house, high above the quickened sound of her own frightened breathing.

"With cold, trembling fingers she reached under the pillow and grabbed frantically for the little flashlight. Quickly she pulled it out, sat up, and snapped the button. She turned its bright beam squarely upon the exact spot where stood her midnight visitor.

"Elsie's eyes stared unbelievingly as the flashlight trembled in her hand. 'It—it isn't true! It can't be true,' she thought. 'If I pinch myself, I'll find I'm dreaming.'

"For Elsie saw that there was no one there— no one at all! The bright flashlight beam revealed only the empty room—only the old-fashioned, quiet room, and nothing more.

"With a terrified moan Elsie dropped the flashlight and fell back upon the pillow. Frantically she pulled the covers over her head and curled under them, shaking and shivering, for what seemed an endless time. She thrust her fingers into her ears to try to shut out the sound of the footsteps as they walked round and round the room.

"Then for a time there was utter silence. Elsie unclenched her stiffened fingers and rubbed them together. She was thankful for even a moment's rest from the awful sound of those tramping footsteps.

"'Why did I ever come to this strange place?' she wailed. 'Oh, how I wish I were safe at home in my own bed.' Elsie felt two salty, burning tears trickle down her cheeks as she choked back a racking sob. 'Dear Father,' she prayed, 'protect me and deliver me from evil—from whatever this awful thing is that can be heard but not seen.'

"Then once again Elsie heard the front door open and close. Again she felt the blast of crisp cold night air that blew through the hallway and followed the footsteps into the room where she lay, almost frozen with fear. Again she heard the footsteps slowly advance into the blackness. But this time Elsie heard a thud as the unknown object struck against the table and a very well-known voice exclaimed, 'Ouch!'

"'Bill!' she exclaimed. Anger swept through her. Quickly she turned the flashlight's shining rays upon a frowning Bill. She saw that he hopped storklike upon one foot while he grasped the injured one in his hands.

"'It serves you right!' she exploded. 'How could you frighten me so! Why, I was almost scared out of my wits. I tried and tried to warn you about that table, but of course you wouldn't listen to me. Of course you wouldn't! You were too busy trying to play your horrid joke.'

"'A joke? Warn me? What on earth are you talking about, Elsie!' Bill stammered. 'You must have had a nightmare. Why, I just now came in the front door. I had to work an extra half hour before the relief operator came on duty. That's why I couldn't get home by midnight. But you sound really frightened. What has happened?'

"'What's happened!' Elsie gasped, holding the bed covers tight around her neck. 'I—well, I don't know *what* happened, but *something* did, Bill. If you didn't come in that front door at the stroke of twelve, I don't know who did, but *someone* did. Maybe you think I've been dreaming, but someone came in that door before you got home.'

"'You're quite right, my dear. Of course some- one came in that door,' said a soft voice from the hallway. 'There. Let's have a little light while we talk.' Mrs. Gray spoke calmly.

"'Now, first of all I must tell you that I'm so sor- ry you were frightened, Elsie. But no harm would have befallen you. I supposed that Bill long ago had told you that many of my 'friends' come here regu- larly to see me and to visit with me. In fact, some- times he visits with them too. They walk through the entire house, but most often they come up- stairs, where I hold small meetings. Then at times they come in here on evenings when I am tired and lie down on that davenport.'

"'Your friends?' Elsie asked fearfully. 'What friends do you mean, Mrs. Gray? This couldn't have been one of them, for I saw no one at all.'

"'You probably wouldn't see my friends, Elsie,' Mrs. Gray said. As she spoke Elsie saw her hostess' eyes glance toward the little Bible. 'You see, they wouldn't be visible to you unless you were in close contact with the spirit world as I am. Since I am a spiritualist medium, I can visit with these friends from the other world.'

"'But we've talked enough for now. Lie down and go to sleep. We can visit in the morning when I will tell you more about my work. I've had some wonderful messages from departed ones who have gone on before us not only from my own loved ones but from strangers who wish to contact their own living relatives and friends.'

"'Sleep!' Elsie felt that she would never be able to sleep in that haunted room. Every time she opened her eyes she was sure she would see a ghost in the parlor. Elsie's face was as white as the snowy pillowcase that framed it; her hands felt almost too nerveless to pick up even as light a weight as the little Bible on the edge of the bed. But as she held the Blessed Book in her hands she felt a comforting returning glow of warmth and security. And then she finally fell asleep for a few brief hours of rest.

"No one was stirring when Elsie roused early the next morning. Quietly she slipped out of bed, dressed rapidly, and repacked her overnight bag. But before closing it she took out her leather writing case and fountain pen. Sitting down, she hastily wrote a note of thanks to her hostess and to Bill.

"'I wonder if any other girl ever wrote a thank-you note for the most terrifying night of her life,' Elsie thought grimly as she signed her name and propped the envelope on the fireplace mantel. 'But I've no one to blame but myself for coming here. The least I can do is to thank them for the concert and for my parlor bedroom, even if it did have a ghost in it.'

"Quickly Elsie put her Bible in her purse, picked up her small handbag and tiptoed down the hallway. Quietly she opened the front door and gently she closed it behind her. Then, on winged feet, she flew down the steps, down the deserted street, and at the nearest stop swung aboard a streetcar.

"Just as the car rounded the corner Elsie turned for a last glimpse of the house she hoped never to see again. As the early morning sunlight sparkled frostily against the big upstairs windows something white flickered there. And though after one startled glance Elsie knew that it was only the lace window curtain flapping in the chilly breeze, she turned her head hastily away.

"She talked to Bill only once after that. Then she thanked him for all his many kindnesses to her. But I guess she made it plain that because of his interest in spiritualism she could never really enjoy going anywhere with him again!"

"Oh, what a ghost story!" cried Stephen. "But why was Elsie afraid to see Bill again, Mother. He'd been nice to her. And those old spirits or whatever they were wouldn't have hurt her, would they?"

"Elsie was very wise to tell Bill good-by, Stephen," mother soberly replied. "According to her belief she felt it wrong to have anything to do with a medium. As she told me the story she quoted Bible verses that proved her position.

"'And when they shall say unto you, Seek unto them that have familiar spirits, and unto wizards that peep, and that mutter: should not a people seek unto their God?'

"'The dead know not any thing.' 'Man lieth down, and riseth not: till the heavens be no more, they shall not awake, nor be raised out of their sleep.'

"A medium in Bible days was called a familiar spirit, and since Mrs. Gray was a medium Elsie wanted to stay far, far away from her seances. She did not want to have anything to do with what she called 'the spirits of devils.'"

Mother turned toward Marilyn, who sat strangely quiet. "Now do you begin to see why I have asked you not to go to this Halloween fortune-telling party, dear? It might be just a harmless prank, but again it might prove to be something far more dangerous. I have always remembered Elsie's story. I hope that you children will always remember it too."

"Thank you, Mother," said Marilyn. "I'm glad you told us the story. And I'm sorry I was so cross about insisting on going to Jane's party. Of course, I wanted to go, but I don't now.

"I'll hurry and write that note this very minute. In fact, I'll hurry almost as much as Elsie did when she wrote her note to Bill and his mother. But at least I'll be safe afterward. I'm glad there's no ghost in our parlor."

Chapter 11
A Date With Death

WELL, Well!" exclaimed George Hibbard. He looked up from his reading rack in glad surprise. "How are you, Harold? Come right over by the bed and say hello to me. Where did you come from, and how did you find me out here in my sister Roberta's country home?"

Harold hurried across the room to smile down at the cheerful paralytic and to remove the reading rack from the bed and place it on a nearby table.

"Thank you very much," said George. "Now sit down where I can see you while you tell me about yourself. It's been some time since you visited me at the Hibbard home in Bums, Oregon. I'm still wondering how you knew that I was staying near Portland this fall."

"Oh, good news travels fast, Mr. Hibbard," Harold laughed. "But, seriously, I found out from one of my school friends who was invited to a meeting of the Oregon Chin-Up Club. He overheard one man ask another if George Hibbard was coming to the party, so of course he inquired about you, as I'd told him of all the good visits you and I had had together. I certainly was glad to learn that you're

For Six Months They Ate and Slept, Fished and Hunted

living so near Portland. I'll be able to come out quite often and see you."

"Indeed, I'd be more than happy to have you too, Harold. However, in just a few days I'll be leaving for Arizona, where I expect to spend the winter in that land of sunshine. It'll certainly be something out of the ordinary for me, after all these years in the Far West.

"But don't look so downhearted. I'll be coming back in the spring, and then I'll probably spend the summer with my sister Hazel, who lives right in Portland. You'll be more than welcome to come there. I'll no doubt have some new stories to tell you by that time."

"That'll be fine," said Harold in a relieved tone. "For just a minute I was afraid you were moving away. If you did, I'd never get to hear that exciting story you mentioned at our last meeting. Do you remember?"

"Of course I do," nodded George. "It was called 'A Date With Death,' and it really is an exciting story to me, for it concerns my father and his narrow escape. If you like, I'll tell it right now, and if we have time, I'll tell you a second story. I'm sure that you'll find both of them interesting, for they both show in a truly wonderful way the real goodness of the human heart."

Harold settled himself comfortably in his chair and then leaned forward expectantly as he saw George Hibbard draw a deep breath and begin his father's story.

"One beautiful spring day in the year 1898, long before I was born, my father sat anxiously in a Portland doctor's office. As he restlessly waited his eyes stared unseeingly through the window that framed majestic, snow-capped Mount Hood. But at that moment he was not interested in the scenery. Instead, he kept thinking, dreading, what the doctor might tell him. Already he had visited five physicians. Each one had said, 'I'm sorry, Dr. Hibbard, but I can give you no hope. There is nothing that I can do for you—nothing at all.'

"But he had made up his mind that he would keep searching until some doctor gave him at least a ray of hope. However, after a careful examination dad's heart sank when he saw the look on this doctor's face and heard him speak.

"'Dr. Hibbard, you've asked for the truth. I must tell you that, if you close your dental office at once and spend most of your time resting out doors, you may live for six months. Both of your lungs are badly infected with tuberculosis; there is nothing that medical science can do to lengthen your life. It is my painful duty to tell you that your days are numbered!'

"Though dad's heart pounded violently and his breath caught in his throat he shook his head firmly and clenched his hands.

"'I can't die, doctor!' he exclaimed. 'No, I *can't* die. Why, I have a wife and two babies who love me and depend upon me. I can't leave them.'

"Somehow he managed to stumble out of the office and reach home, where he fell upon his bed, completely exhausted. But even then, in the back of his mind, a dim plan was forming—a plan that he felt offered a glimmer of hope."

"What was it, Mr. Hibbard? Did your father know of a cure for tuberculosis?" Harold could not help interrupting. He leaned forward eagerly in his chair, eyes wide and lips parted.

"No, Harold, my father knew very little about tuberculosis and its cure. You must remember that all this happened long before the days of modern medicine. But he knew that he had everything to gain by his experiment and that if it failed he would lose his life. And, since the doctors had offered him no hope, he determined to carry out his plan.

"Dad's courage was at a low ebb when he was forced to lease his dental office. He had worked hard for his education. He and my mother had had high hopes for his future in the dental profession, but now it seemed to him that all his struggles had been in vain.

"After leaving my mother and two sisters with relatives, dad spent the summer at Yachats, by the Pacific Ocean. In the fall he traveled to La Grande, a town in eastern Oregon's higher altitude. During the winter months he stayed with his sister, Helen, who was teaching school there.

"One spring afternoon dad heard a rap at the door. 'It's probably a peddler,' he thought. 'However, I'm too tired to get up and find out.' But once again the knocking sounded, a little louder than at first.

"'All right, all right. Just be patient. I'm coming,' he muttered, stumbling sleepily to the front door.

He was speechless for an instant when he saw who stood there.

"'Why, Shelley Morgan!' he cried. 'Where in the world did you come from? I thought you were in Portland, Oregon. What are you doing up here? Come in, man. Come in and sit down. Let me look at you. You're just a ghost of your former self! What's wrong?'

"'You're just a mere skeleton yourself, doc,' wheezed Shelley; 'so I guess that makes ghosts out of both of us. As for myself, I've come over to stay with you while we keep our date with death. You see, the doctors told me that there is no known cure for this particular type of asthma that's choking me. But I can't just lie down and die like a quitter so I came over to try this high, dry altitude too. I've certainly got nothing to lose by making the change, and I've life itself to gain if my hunch works out.'

"Day after day the two friends met and wondered desperately what they could do to save their lives. They talked about going to the Bitterroot Mountains of Idaho, known to sportsmen for their fine hunting. But they were told that the thick snows blanketing that area would not melt until midsummer. They both knew that they could not wait that long. Already the sands of time had long since run past the six months given them by the doctors.

"'I've finally found a place where we can go,' dad announced one morning to his good friend, Shelley. 'It'll be rugged, and I guess it'll really kill or cure, but who are we to fear any risk with death itself staring us in the face?

"'Several sportsmen have told me to go over the Blue Mountains of eastern Oregon and cross Harney Valley to Harney and Malheur lakes. They told me glowing tales of the bird hunting at the lakes and the fine fishing and hunting in the wild regions of the Steens Mountains. They said that it was surely the place for us. What do you say?'

"'I say yes,' nodded Shelley. 'I'll go out right now and see if I can dicker for a team and wagon for the long journey.'

"'Good! I'll attend to the camp outfit,' dad replied. 'We'll need plenty of food and other supplies. Stores will be mighty few and far between. We'll hurry and leave as soon as possible.'

"What a pitiful sight it must have been when that team and wagon pulled out of La Grande with those two skeleton-thin passengers, both men struggling for lung-filling breaths of pure, clean air. And it must have been a nightmare journey over those long miles and miles of muddy roads, up steep grades and down high mountains. But somehow they kept on and on, until at last they reached the Steens Mountains. And here they stayed, resting in one spot for a few days, then journeying a few miles to make a new camp.

"Dad was determined to build up his strength. In order to do this, he would tax himself to the breaking point, whereupon he would collapse, and his faithful friend would somehow get him back to camp. For six months they ate and slept, fished and hunted. In all this time they had neither a roof over their heads nor a floor beneath their feet—only the arching blue sky overhead and the lush grasses of Harney Valley underfoot.

"I remember that dad used to tell us about his first sight of rye grass. It grew as high as the wagon, and it looked so green and tempting that he made quite an effort to cut some for the horses, only to find that they wouldn't touch it. He used to tell us of the times that he lay resting high on one of the many rocky ledges overhanging the wild, deep gorges of the Steens Mountains. There he would stay quietly for hours and watch the large herds of deer—some with as many as almost sixty—and see how the bucks chose their mates and took them away. At other times he watched the fast-running herds of antelope and the spirited wild horses who galloped swiftly across the wide meadows near the Donner und Blitzen River.

"He also told us of the high water of that spring of 1899, when the waves from the lakes lapped near Charley Haines's little store at the Narrows. Dad got out his canvas rowboat, fixed the wooden ribs to hold it rigid for use, and rowed out into the deep channel about two hundred yards from shore to get some shooting. Just as he lifted his gun he was horrified to feel the boat's wooden ribs collapsing. His heart seemed to jump into his throat and choke him as he struggled desperately in the cold waves.

"'Am I to die this way?' he thought wildly. Then, as he recalled the many stories told of the lake's great unmeasured depth, his arms and legs thrashed about even more strongly. But at last he saw that it was no use.

"Just as he began sinking his knee struck against some hidden object. Dad gave one last frantic lurch and found to his astonishment that his knees were actually scraping against the muddy bottom of the lake bed. The water had not been more than waist deep all the way! After he rested awhile on the shore he waded back out to the scene of the accident and rescued his boat and his gun."

"But did your father get well?" Harold asked quickly. "Did his trip to the Steens Mountains actually save his life?"

"A little arithmetic would tell you that, Harold," laughed George Hibbard, "for I wasn't born until 1913. However, I won't keep you waiting for the outcome of the story."

"Dad and Shelley Morgan returned to Portland in the fall of 1899. Dad had been gone just a year. As soon as he had spent a few days with mother and the children he returned to the last doctor whom he had visited in the spring of 1898. Once again he waited impatiently in the doctor's office. But this time his eyes stared straight at beautiful Mount Hood.

"'All my life I'll love mountains,' dad thought. "'I will lift up mine eyes unto the hills, from whence cometh my help." Without those hard months in the mountains I wouldn't be here now.'

"When dad entered the inner office the doctor rose from his chair and said, 'Just a minute, sir. I believe that Dr. Hibbard is ahead of you.'

"'I am Dr. Hibbard,' smiled lean, bronzed dad, grasping the doctor's outstretched hand.

125

"*'You* are Dr. Hibbard? It can't be possible!' the physician exclaimed unbelievingly. He was so amazed that he could only shake his head wonderingly as he examined dad and pronounced him well on the road to recovery.

"'If you will move to a higher climate and spend at least one half of your time in the open air each day, you should completely recover your health. Dr. Hibbard, you should thank your lucky star for this miracle.'

"'No, not my lucky star,' dad said soberly. 'I owe my recovery to the unselfish faith and courage of a true friend—and to God.'

"Dad sold his Portland dental practice that fall and brought his little family to eastern Oregon. In the biting cold of November they traveled for two days and nights from Ontario to Burns, Oregon. His first dental office in Burns was in a little room in the old French Hotel, operated by Madame Racine. Finally he built his own office building, which in later years he was glad to turn over to my brother Llewellyn, who is also a dentist. There in our Burns home on the hill, where you used to visit me in the summertime, the rest of our family were born: Llewellyn, Hazel, Hal, Frances, I, and Virginia.

"But, true to his promise to the physician, dad always spent half a day out in the open air. You remember the stories that I have told you of the coyotes in 'King and Queen Go Hunting,' the antelope fawn of 'Desert Capture,' and the eaglets in 'The Nest of Gold'? They best show dad's genuine love for the outdoors. Throughout the years he became more and more interested in saving wild-life. Finally he was made a member of the Oregon State Game Commission. He became an authority on the birds and wild game of Oregon, and he always had an interesting story to tell attentive listeners. Many important people became his friends, but dad always remained the same, a friend to rich and poor alike."

"What an exciting story!" Harold exclaimed. "But what happened to Shelley Morgan? Did he get well too?"

"Stranger than fiction, both dad and Shelley lived to be eighty years of age. They long outlived all the doctors who had given them 'a date with death.' And neither of them ever forgot the miracle that true friendship had accomplished.

"But there! I'd intended to tell you about my own wonderful surprise this last October," George ended, "for without this surprise I wouldn't be able to take this trip. However, I see that it's too late now to do so. But I promise that I'll tell you all about it the next time I see you, either before I leave for Arizona or after I return. So until then, Harold, I'll say goodby. And I'll look forward to meeting you again and to telling you about my unexpected 'Christmas in October!'"

We invite you to view the complete
selection of titles we publish at:

www.TEACHServices.com

Scan with your mobile
device to go directly
to our website.

Please write or email us your praises, reactions, or
thoughts about this or any other book we publish at:

TEACH Services, Inc.
PUBLISHING
www.TEACHServices.com • (800) 367-1844

P.O. Box 954
Ringgold, GA 30736

info@TEACHServices.com

TEACH Services, Inc., titles may be purchased in bulk
for educational, business, fund-raising, or sales pro-
motional use. For information, please e-mail:

BulkSales@TEACHServices.com

Finally, if you are interested in seeing
your own book in print, please contact us at

publishing@TEACHServices.com

We would be happy to review your manuscript for free.

CPSIA information can be obtained at www.ICGtesting.com
Printed in the USA
BVOW03s0623091014

370079BV00007B/111/P